DRUM ROLL, PLEASE

DRUM ROLL, PLEASE

LISA JENN BIGELOW

HARPER

An Imprint of HarperCollinsPublishers

Library of Congress Control Number: 2018933338
ISBN 978-0-06-279114-6
Typography by Michelle Cunningham
18 19 20 21 22   CG/LSCH   10 9 8 7 6 5 4 3 2 1
❖

First Edition

Dedicated to Joe—
Melly wouldn't have been a drummer
without you

DRUM
ROLL,
PLEASE

one

The Camp Rockaway brochure promised every kid was a rock star waiting to happen, but they never met me. We hadn't even arrived, and I was ready to turn around and go home. My heart beat faster and faster, like the world's worst metronome, until it froze—until I couldn't feel or think or breathe. Then, just when it felt like nothing but a jumble of clockwork bits, it stuttered to life again.

Mom's car zipped along the highway. Billboards dwindled by the minute, farmland giving way to forest the farther north we went. In the back seat, my best friend, Olivia, leaned over and whispered, for what had to be the fifth time, "Are you sure you're okay?"

I shrugged. I hadn't cried in over an hour. That had to count for something, right?

She squeezed my hand. "You're going to get through

this. Only two weeks, and I'll be with you the whole time. We'll rock so hard you'll forget the rest of the world exists."

I nodded. I couldn't expect Olivia to understand.

She wasn't the one who'd woken up yesterday to the sweet smell of Dad's homemade waffles and fresh-squeezed orange juice—like it was somebody's birthday, except it wasn't, which should've tipped me off. She wasn't the one whose parents had, at the end of break-fast, announced, "We've decided we're better off apart." She hadn't shuffled like a zombie through the past twenty-four hours as Mom took her shopping for a new swimsuit and Dad scanned apartment listings on his phone.

It wasn't the next two weeks I was worried about. It was the rest of my life.

I knew Olivia had more to say, but we couldn't talk about anything important on the ride because Mom was right there. Instead, we sang along to the radio and talked about music. Which is to say, Olivia talked. She always knew who'd put out a new album, who was dat-ing whom, who'd trashed a hotel room, who'd checked into rehab. She sucked up gossip like a sponge.

I only half heard what she was saying, my eyes stuck on the empty seat next to Mom. Dad was sup-posed to be sitting there, singing "Crazy on You" in an off-key falsetto and passing around the road atlas to see who could find the funniest town names: Sweet Lips, Tennessee, or Elephant Butte, New Mexico. Instead he was back in Kalamazoo, looking for a new place to live.

The scenery along the highway faded, and I was back in the kitchen, morning sun streaming through the window. I'd dropped my fork with a clatter, and it lay dripping syrup on the white tile floor. My tuxedo cat, Maki, licked at it cautiously. "We both love you very much," Mom said as I stared. "We want you to know you absolutely did not do anything wrong."

I knew that! But you don't just wake up and say, *Good morning, honey, let's eat waffles and get divorced.* It's not like I was expecting a drum roll, but shouldn't there have been a sign something big was coming? Where had the arguments been, the screaming, the glares and cold shoulders? The signs that something was terribly wrong? I searched my memory and came up empty. The night before, they'd finished a crossword together.

"But why?" I'd croaked.

They'd exchanged a glance. Dad said, "It's because—" at the same time Mom said, "That's not important right now, sweetie." And we listened to seconds tick by on the clock, the one shaped like a flying chicken, with fried eggs on the hands, that Dad picked out at the art fair one summer. He'd picked it out, but Mom had laughed, too, imagining it on our wall. We'd laughed so hard.

How could this be happening? And why the day before I left for camp?

Maybe I shouldn't have been so surprised about that part. My parents always had the worst timing. Like when Dad told me Grandma Goodwin was in the hospital with a fractured hip ten minutes before my pre-algebra test. I got a D, I was so distracted. Or when I was six and Mom slipped the truth about Santa on Christmas Eve. I cried myself to sleep and refused to open my presents in the morning. They sat wrapped under the tree until December 26.

I couldn't believe they expected me to pack my suitcase as if everything were normal. But Mom said, "Trust me, Melly Mouse, by the time you're back home, the news will have sunk in, and we'll all be ready to talk calmly and rationally about what this means for the future."

Calm and rational. Like this conversation? She was like a newscaster reporting a devastating earthquake. The entire studio could be crashing down around our heads, and she'd read the headlines in a pleasant voice, ignoring the dust and debris raining on her suit. At least Dad looked sorry, every part of him drooping, from his round shoulders to his black mustache.

I knocked back my chair, sending Maki skittering from the room, and stumbled, blind with tears, to the basement where my drums were. I played as hard and fast as I could, all the loudest, most-likely-to-aggravate-my-parents songs Olivia had loaded onto my phone. My right foot on the bass drum was the boom of thunder. The hi-hat sizzled like lightning. My sticks rolled across the toms like rain on the roof, clattered across the cymbals like hail on the window. For a wonderful time, the rest of the world was washed away. There was only music, with me in the eye of the storm.

But in the end—when my phone died and my arms grew sore and I really had to pee—I'd had to climb those stairs again. Quietly I packed my suitcase. Without drums, Melly Mouse was just that: a mouse. And now, like it or not, I was on my way to camp.

Mom caught my eye in the rearview mirror. Her forehead creased. I looked away. At least she had the decency not to smile at me.

We turned from the highway onto a curving country road, swooping over low hills, past marshes and prairie. Then, a few miles later, onto a bumpy dirt road lined by tall trees—hundreds of them, thousands, placed so thick I couldn't see what lay past them.

"I didn't expect there to be so many trees." The words tumbled out of me.

Olivia said, "Of course there are trees. It's camp. What were you expecting?"

"I'm not sure." Not this, this crush of green all around us.

"Camp equals woods. Woods equals trees," Olivia said.

"I know," I said. "But I've never seen trees like this."

"Yeah," Olivia said, softer. "Me neither."

Neither of us had really spent time in the Great Outdoors—capital G, capital O. In Kalamazoo, trees stood in well-behaved lines along the parkways and held tire swings in people's backyards. Aside from field trips to the nature center, to walk around the bog and see rehabilitated owls and turtles, the wildest place I'd ever been was the Grand Canyon—and that was about as far opposite the woods of northern Michigan as you could get.

We turned once more, and the road opened up into a bright parking lot. Gravel grumbled under the tires. Dust puffed up in clouds. Mom always ran early, but it seemed everyone else was just as eager. As we parked, car after car pulled in around us.

I dipped my forehead against the window, staring without meaning to. I'd be here for two whole weeks with these people, and I didn't even know a thing about them. Every car was like a package on the front step, what was inside a mystery.

Olivia had already thrown open her door. I slowly followed her into the hot, muggy July air. Mom popped the trunk and started heaving luggage onto the packed dirt. A suitcase, sleeping bag, pillow, and mosquito netting for each of us, plus Olivia's bass guitar.

Camp Rockaway provided drums, amps, and plenty of other instruments and gear, but there was no way Olivia would settle for anyone's bass but her own. It was fretless, and stained the color of cherry cough drops. When Olivia's fingers danced along the neck, her dark hair swishing in time to the music, she looked like a real rock star. And that was *before* Camp Rockaway.

My only gear was my leather stick bag, which I slung over my shoulder.

"Ouch!" Olivia cried, hopping around and slapping at her ankle. "Something bit me."

"Hold on," Mom said. She fumbled in her handbag and pulled out a bottle of bug spray. There was another bottle somewhere in my suitcase. Olivia squirted herself.

The air was thick with the sound of bugs I didn't recognize. I knew the whine of mosquitoes, the buzz of houseflies. This was a whole orchestra. It hummed in my ears, pulsed in my brain. My skin vibrated like the skin of a drum. My fingers flexed as if grasping imaginary sticks. For the first time in over a day, I forgot what was going on at home.

Mom waved the bug spray at me. "You'd better put some on, too, Melly."

At her voice, I remembered everything and frowned.

As I rubbed repellent on my arms and legs, I watched a white taxicab roll into the lot and lurch to a stop. It looked out of place amid the minivans and SUVs. A girl with tawny brown skin and dark brown hair braided into rows jumped out of the passenger seat. The driver opened the trunk. He pulled out a large duffel bag, bedding, mosquito netting, and an acoustic guitar. It was in a cheap case, the black cardboard kind, covered with stickers.

Who came to camp in a taxi? Where were her parents? The girl handed the driver money and shook his hand, as if it were an everyday thing for her. As she turned from him, she saw me watching. She smiled at me—a big, braces-flashing smile.

I blushed and looked away. I needed a shirt for times like this. It would say, *Don't mind me, I'm just socially awkward.* I handed the bug spray back to my mother.

"No, you keep it," Mom said. "If it's this buggy all the time, I want you to have extra."

The girl from the taxi walked past us. I sneaked a look at the stickers on her guitar case. "Peace Love Music." "More cowbell." "WUPX: The pulse of the UP." "This machine kills fascists." I didn't get that one at all.

I remembered from our World War II unit that Mussolini was a fascist, but I couldn't remember how he'd died. Still, I was pretty sure it had nothing to do with guitars.

It didn't seem possible she could carry all her luggage at once, but there was her duffel across her back. There were her sleeping bag and netting in one hand, her guitar case in the other. If she felt weighed down by all that stuff, you couldn't tell. She looked as carefree as if she were carrying a bundle of balloons. As if she had only to wish it, and she'd skim across the parking lot, her toes barely stirring up swirls of dust. I couldn't help staring as she floated away.

A small voice inside me said, *Remember, your life is in pieces. You shouldn't be here. You should be at home, under the covers, crying.*

But another voice chanted louder, merging with the chorus of bugs in the trees, *Forget, forget, forget.*

two

We towed our luggage across the lot to the growing mob of campers and their families. Sprinkled in were Camp Rockaway staff wearing black T-shirts and holding clipboards. A woman with wispy blond hair, glasses, and a sunburned nose made her way over.

"Hi, welcome to Camp Rockaway!" she said. "I'm Poppy. Let me get your names, and we can figure out where you're headed."

"Olivia Mendoza," Olivia said.

"What do you know?" Poppy said, making a checkmark on her clipboard. "You'll be camping up in Treble Cliff with me." She turned to me. "What about you?"

"Melissa Goodwin," Olivia said, before I had even processed the question.

"Looks like you're in Treble Cliff, too. Welcome, Melissa. Wait, I see a note here that you go by a nickname." Poppy pushed up her glasses and squinted at the page. "Sorry, Damon—our director—has terrible handwriting."

I thought about telling her, yes, I did have a nickname: Lissa. Lissa sounded so much more sophisticated than Melly. A name for a rock star, not a mouse.

Then Olivia said, "She's Melly!" and that little fantasy fizzled out.

Oh, well. It's not like I would've had the guts to say something anyway.

"Melly. Olivia. Terrific. You two can put your stuff over by that post. The ranger will drive it to the campsite. Hold on to any personal instruments until after your audition."

My stomach twisted. This was the first I'd heard anything about an audition.

Poppy saw my panic. "Don't be scared. We call it an audition, but it's more of an interview. It's our way of learning a little bit about you. Nobody's judging you. Nobody gets sent home for not being good enough. Okay?"

She pulled out some maps from under her clipboard and began making circles and X's. "We're here. The practice cabins are where the auditions take place. Afterward you can take your instruments up to the lodge. We've got lockers there. Finally, here's Treble

Cliff. It's a bit of a hike, I know, but it's gorgeous up there. The best campsite at Camp Rockaway."

She grinned as she handed the maps to Olivia and me. "See you up there."

We found the post for Treble Cliff, one in a line of eight. There was one for Bass Cliff, too, of course, and for Carole Kingdom and Buddy Hollow. Each name was punnier than the last. Olivia and I rolled our eyes as Mom chuckled. I felt a pang. I wished Dad had been the one to drive us. Nobody appreciated a good (or bad, depending on how you looked at it) pun like Dad. We piled up our things, pillows balanced on top of sleeping bags on top of suitcases to keep them out of the dust.

Mom snatched my map. "This way to the practice cabins," she said, and started walking.

My feet stuck to the ground. "Um, Mom? I don't think you're supposed to go with us."

"What do you mean, Melly? Of course I'm going with you." She waved the map toward the trail. "Look at all these parents going with their kids."

Olivia and I exchanged a glance, as if to say, *Should you tell her, or should I?*

Olivia gave a polite cough. "Only the little kids," she said.

"Oh, good grief," Mom said, but she looked around and saw what we'd seen: all the other kids our age were already hugging their parents good-bye. SUVs and minivans were backing out of their spaces to make room for the next round of arrivals.

Mom sighed. "Are you sure, Melly?"

I wasn't, not really. Once Mom left, Olivia and my sticks would be the only familiar things I could hold on to. But I couldn't show up to my audition with my mother in tow. I had enough to worry about without the other campers thinking I was a scared little mama's girl.

"I'm sure," I said. "We'll be fine. You can go."

"Yes, we'll be fine," Olivia said. "I promise we won't get lost. I'm an excellent navigator."

She reached for the map, and for a second I thought Mom wasn't going to let go. Her grip tightened, rumpling the paper's edge. Suddenly it slipped from her fingers. Mom looked sad, and I wondered if she was thinking about driving home to an empty house. Well, that was her fault—hers and Dad's. I refused to feel sorry for her.

"Fine. I'll go," Mom said. "But only because you two can't start camp in a state of humiliation. I can't have that on my conscience." She drew me into a hug. I stood stiffly at first, but then instinct kicked in, and I sank into her soft embrace.

"Use lots of sunscreen," she said into my neck. "Your fair skin burns so easily."

"Okay, Mom."

"Eat your fruits and vegetables. Don't stay up all night talking."

"Okay, Mom."

"And write, please. I put some stationery in the pocket of your suitcase, and some envelopes—already stamped. If you want to write to your father, I'll make sure he gets it. I know he'd love to hear from you, too."

This time I didn't answer. I didn't want to make a promise I wasn't sure I could keep.

Fortunately, Olivia chose that moment to say, "I need a hug, too, Mrs. Goodwin!"

Mom released me and held out her arms to Olivia. "Come here, and give me a squeeze." Their embrace was so uncomplicated. Nothing was changing between the two of them.

Suddenly I wondered if the divorce meant Mom would change her name. It was sort of old-fashioned that she'd changed it to match Dad's in the first place. But she'd been Mrs. Goodwin all my life. Was she going to be Ms. Schiff from now on?

And what would happen to *my* name now that Dad was moving out? Would I stay Melly Goodwin, or would I become Melly Schiff? Would I even have any say in the matter?

"One more hug, and I swear I'll go," Mom said. She hugged me so hard I was pretty sure there'd be finger marks on my ribs. "Have fun," she whispered. "Don't worry about Dad and me. Just think about yourself, and I'll see you in two weeks, sunshine. I love you."

I think she was waiting for me to say *I love you* back, but I didn't. Finally she let go, kissed me on the cheek, and turned toward the parking lot.

"Wait!" I called. She turned back eagerly, but all I said was, "Pet Maki for me."

She smiled, but it looked pasted on. "I will. I'll give him lots of extra playing with his feather toy." Then she disappeared into the crowd.

Olivia and I watched her go. Olivia said, "Well, I guess camp's officially begun!"

"I guess so," I said, and pasted on my own smile.

We walked along a shady trail that must have been packed down by thousands of campers. After a while it spilled into a grassy clearing with six small, windowless cabins arranged in a hexagon. Muffled music escaped and blurred in the open air. Campers lined up outside. As we joined them, one of the doors opened, and a boy carrying a guitar case came out, looking happy. A counselor stuck his head out and called for the next camper.

"Why does that cabin say Plymouth on the door?" Olivia said as it shut again.

"I don't know," I said. "Why does that one say Gibraltar?"

"Plymouth is the rock where the Pilgrims landed, right?" Olivia frowned. "What do Pilgrims have to do with anything?"

"Who knows?" I said. "Gibraltar's somewhere in Europe. There's a big rock there—oh!"

Olivia got the joke at the same time I did. She rolled her eyes. "Plymouth Rock. Rock of Gibraltar. *Somebody* thinks they're hilarious."

I read the signs on the other doors: Uluru, Zuma, Guatapé, and Trolltunga. Presumably they were other famous rocks around the world. Dad would be so bummed to have missed this! I'd have to tell him—assuming I ever felt like speaking to him again.

"What do you want to bet Trolltunga means 'troll tongue'?" Olivia said.

"Can I bet you're probably right?" I asked.

The door to Uluru opened, and a counselor beckoned to Olivia. "Wish me luck!" she said.

"Luck," I said, as if she needed it. Me, on the other hand . . .

It's not like I was a terrible drummer. I wasn't amazing, but considering I'd learned most of what I knew from online videos, I thought I did okay. But there was a huge difference between playing alone in my basement, or even with Olivia, and performing for a complete stranger. It didn't matter that Poppy had promised it wasn't a test. My hands felt like wilted lettuce.

"Next!" a voice called sharply. A tall, thin woman with olive skin and jagged black hair was waiting for me at the door to one of the cabins—Trolltunga. Of course I got the cabin named after a piece of troll anatomy. It seemed like a bad omen. I hesitated, and the kid in line behind me poked me between my shoulder blades. I stumbled forward.

The counselor closed the door behind me. "I'm Donna. Have a seat." When I moved toward the folding chair by the door, she added with a smirk, "At the drums. You *are* a drummer, aren't you?"

I guess the stick bag gave me away. Embarrassed, I obeyed.

"I'll try to make this as painless as possible," Donna said. "Name?" Just like Poppy, she had a clipboard and pen. Unlike Poppy's blue Bic, Donna's pen was decorated with skulls.

"Melly—Melissa Goodwin."

"How long have you been playing?"

I counted back in my head. "Almost three years. I mean, that's when I started band at school. But I just played bass drum at first. And then in sixth grade I mostly played snare. I didn't get my drum set until—"

Donna waved her hand like she was shooing a fly.

I wondered why she'd asked the question if she didn't want to hear the answer. "What kind of music do you like to play? What are your favorite bands?"

"Um. Anything," I said. "I mean, usually other people choose. I just play along."

"Okay. But what would you choose if you were the leader of the band?"

I squirmed. Leader of the band? That would never happen. Even when I played alone, I used songs from the playlists Olivia put together. "I don't know," I told Donna. "I guess I just like making noise."

It sounded silly, but it was true.

It all started in the fall of fifth grade, when Olivia dragged me to Ms. Estrada's instrument petting zoo. Ms. Estrada mostly taught middle school band, but she came to our school two afternoons a week to teach the fifth graders. The petting zoo was how she recruited new members. From flute to French horn, from tuba to tom-toms, she laid out every instrument around the music room for us to touch. If it didn't involve saliva, we could even play it.

"How about you on trumpet, me on trombone?" Olivia said. "Or me on oboe, you on clarinet?"

I hadn't told her I had no intention of joining band. My DNA didn't include a single musical gene. I could barely creak out "Happy Birthday." I edged my way around the room, letting the other kids wrestle over the tenor sax, which was quickly established as the coolest instrument, and the metallophone, which sounded good without even trying.

Somehow I ended up alone with the bass drum. It hulked in the very back of the room, looking less like a musical instrument than an uncomfortable piece of furniture. Maybe that's why it had been overlooked. Its wooden body must have gleamed once, but now it was scratched and scuffed. Its skins were dappled gray from being struck countless times. It was no tenor sax.

It's stupid, but I remember thinking, *No one is watching. I can hit this drum, and no one will know it was me.* My fingers curled around the mallet, a stick topped with rabbit-tail fluff. I lifted it high and swung it as hard as I could.

As it made contact, vibrations sizzled up my arm and rattled my teeth. The drum released a *WOGGA-WOGGA-WOGGA* so loud and deep I felt it in my stomach. Of course, everyone immediately turned to stare. Ms. Estrada's fingers were in her ears.

I hated people looking at me, but I couldn't help it: I got a wild smile on my face. That drum had sung louder and truer than I ever could myself. I was dazed. I was dazzled. I wrote my name in capital letters under "Percussion" on the sign-up sheet.

Olivia was even more excited. "I'll sign up to play guitar. We can start our own band!"

"Oh," I said, my stomach feeling weird for some reason. "I thought you were picking oboe or trombone. Is guitar even an option?"

"It will be," Olivia said breezily. "I'll work it out with Ms. Estrada."

"But since when do you have a guitar?"

She shrugged. "My birthday's next month, and my grandfather told me to think about what I want. Well, I've decided I want a guitar! It's okay with you, right?"

"Sure!" I said. "Starting a band would be awesome, I guess. I just hadn't thought that far ahead." The truth was I hadn't thought past playing that bass drum again.

Olivia hugged me. "We're going to be rock stars someday, Melly. You wait and see."

And I guess I caught her excitement, because suddenly I felt all right again.

Still, you can't play rock when your entire musical career consists of whacking a bass drum, no matter how good your time or your tone is. It took a couple of years of school band to convince my parents drums weren't just a phase, and Olivia did more than her share of wheedling in the meantime. But one day they surprised me with an old drum set they'd bought on Craigslist. Who cared that the black veneer was covered with stickers from eighties hair bands? It was mine. I could make the house shake.

We'd ride our bikes to my house after school, Olivia's guitar strapped to her back. Sometimes our friends joined us, Todd on his own electric, Stella on vocals and synths. But mostly it was the two of us, playing hour after hour, everything from the Rolling Stones to Tegan and Sara—whatever Olivia had scrounged up.

This past year, she added bass to her repertoire. "We don't need two electric players," she said. "What we do need is a rhythm section." A rhythm section: bass and drums, holding down the beat, keeping the band on track—together.

And now we were at Camp Rockaway.

"Tell you what," Donna said, and maybe it was paranoia, but I thought I heard her give a little sigh. "I'm going to play something on guitar"—she leaned over and grabbed an acoustic from where it was propped against the wall—"and you jump in and play along. Okay?"

I pulled a pair of sticks from my bag. As Donna began to strum in four-four time, a song that could have been any song, I joined in with a simple rock beat. My right foot worked the bass drum pedal on one and three. My left hand answered on the snare drum, with rim shots on two and four. My right arm stretched across my body to the hi-hat: *tap-tap-tap-tap-tap-tap-tap-tap*. . . .

"Keep going."

My playing was so stiff I sounded like a robot. I forced myself to play a little louder, as if increasing the volume would pump up the energy. It sort of worked, but my hands still shook. I reached up for my cymbals, hoping a good, solid crash would cover my nerves.

"Give me a fill."

Hesitantly I rolled my sticks across the toms from high to low and back again. When I played back home, all of me—my body, my head, my heart—belonged to the music. The music filled me to the brim. There was no room for anything else. But here, playing for a scowling stranger with a skull pen and clipboard, I was so full of worry there was hardly any room for the music. My sticks caught on the drum heads, ruining the rhythm. Only my foot on the bass drum pedal was steady.

But thinking about my foot was a mistake. It fumbled. I tried to find the beat again, but I'd lost it. I bit my lip. The only way this moment could be worse was if I started to cry.

"You can stop," Donna said, scribbling on the clipboard. "I've got what I need."

I sat frozen. Could that really be it? I tried to read Donna's face, but she didn't look up. I stood and walked past her to the door.

Outside Trolltunga, Olivia grabbed me. "How'd it go,

Melly? Easy-peasy, right? I can't wait until tomorrow, when we actually get to play in a band. They should've auditioned us together, so they'd know what kind of a rhythm section they're really getting."

I tried to match her enthusiasm, but my stomach knotted. If everyone made the cut at Camp Rockaway, why did I feel like such a failure?

three

Treble Cliff lived up to its name. As we climbed the steep, pine-needled path, I was huffing and puffing. Olivia's forehead shone. She shook out her hair and scooped it into a fresh ponytail. I wished I could do the same, but last week the stylist had cut mine exactly the wrong length: long enough to make my neck hot but too short to pull back.

"At least I didn't have to carry my bass all the way up here," Olivia said. After leaving our auditions, we'd followed the map to the lodge, where she'd picked out a locker.

"Cardio's good for you," I said, panting.

"Not dying of a heart attack is good for me," Olivia said, and stopped, because waiting for us at the top of the hill was yet another counselor with yet another clipboard.

"Oh," I said, at the same time as Olivia said, "Nice."

The counselor had spiky blue hair. Rings went up the sides of both her ears, and she had more rings in her eyebrow and her nose. I wondered if she was hidden way back here in the woods so she didn't scare off the touchier parents. But her round face was friendly. "Hey," she said, "I'm Blair. Whom do I have the pleasure—"

"Olivia and Melly," Olivia said.

"Let me guess." Blair chewed her pen. "Drummer, obviously," she said, pointing at my stick bag, "and I'm gonna say lead guitar." She jerked her chin at Olivia.

Olivia beamed. "Bass, actually, for camp purposes. But believe me, I am all about leading from behind."

"I'll just bet," Blair said. "Tents are starting to fill up, but you should still have your pick. Any of the yellow ones. Blue's for staff. The ranger'll be by with his truck any minute. He'll drop your stuff at the bottom of the hill."

I couldn't help it. I groaned.

Blair's lips twitched. "It's the price we pay for this primo real estate. Everyone knows this is the best site at Camp Rockaway. Take a sec and look around."

We did. We were surrounded by towering pines. The treetops framed a circle of brilliant turquoise sky. I got dizzy staring up—a good kind of dizzy.

"At night," Blair said, "that break in the trees is a tunnel to the freaking stars." She let that sink in before adding with a wink, "Plus if it storms, all the water runs downhill to Carole Kingdom. Go on, now. Pick out your tent."

When I first heard we were going to stay in tents, I'd imagined flimsy pup tents staked to the ground, roots and rocks poking up through our sleeping bags. Olivia had shown me photos on Camp Rockaway's website proving otherwise, but they hadn't prepared me for the real thing. They were big and made of bulky canvas, rigged on wooden frames off the ground. Through the open flaps, I could see four cots set up on each tent's plank floor.

"There's people in that one, that one, that one . . ." Olivia ticked them off on her fingers.

"In other words, there's people in all of them," I said.

"How do we know which one to choose?"

"What are you afraid of?" I teased. "That we'll end up with someone who snores?"

Olivia had a deviated septum. When she fell asleep, it sounded like someone was revving up a chainsaw. She threw me a dirty look. But when I crossed my eyes at her, she laughed.

"End of the line," Olivia said as we approached the final tent.

Sitting on the front steps was a freckled girl with glasses and spirals of reddish brown hair, playing a harmonica. Her song chugged along cheerfully as her lips skated along the silver surface. She lowered it when she saw us. "Hey."

"Hey, sorry to interrupt. Do you have two empty beds?" Olivia asked.

"I've got three." The girl unfolded herself and stood up. I wasn't short, but I barely came up to her shoulder. "I'm Shauna," she said. "You two are first-timers, right?"

"Olivia," Olivia said, pointing to herself, "and Melly. It's that obvious we're new?"

"There's something in your faces. Your eyes are, like, extra big." Shauna grinned.

"You play harmonica?" I asked. As if what we'd seen and heard before was a hallucination. *C-minus in conversational skills, Melly.*

Shauna said, "Yep. And guitar. I'm a country girl. Or I should say, country woman. Women in country music are infantilized enough without me doing it to myself."

"Infantilized?" Olivia asked.

"Oh, you know. Men singing, 'I wanna go down by the river with my sweet little girl and drink whiskey on the Fourth of July.' That kind of thing. If they're drinking whiskey with actual little girls, they're pedophiles."

I had no idea what to make of Shauna, but I was pretty sure I liked her.

"What about you two?" she asked. "Drums, of course." She nodded at my stick bag.

There it was again. At Camp Rockaway, everyone knew just by looking at me how I spent my free time. Back home, most people thought my stick bag was an ugly purse.

"I play guitar and bass," Olivia told her, "but I only brought my bass."

Shauna nodded. "Wise choice. There's always an army of guitar players."

"Luggage!" Blair bellowed across the campsite. "Get your luggage, bottom of the hill."

"Oh boy." Olivia sighed. "Do we actually need any of that stuff? Maybe we can leave it there for the next two weeks, and the ranger can pick it up again before we go home."

"Did you bring mosquito netting?" Shauna asked. "You'll want that, for sure. My first time at camp, I made the mistake of going without. I had so many mosquito bites by the time I went home, my parents didn't recognize me."

I had the feeling her mosquito bites would've blended right in with her freckles, but point taken. I had no interest in being a bunch of mosquitoes' all-night buffet. "Come on," I told Olivia. "Cardio, remember? When we get back to school, we'll get A's in PE for sure."

"I'll go with you," Shauna said. "There's no use post-poning the inevitable."

On our way down, we passed other girls coming up with their gear. The girl from the taxi was one of them. "Hello again," she said as we brushed past each other on the path. I managed only a startled *hi* before she was gone, up the hill.

"Who was that?" Olivia asked. "She acted like she knew you."

I shook my head. "How could she? We just got here."

"Maybe you've got friends here you haven't told me about," Olivia joked.

"Secret rock-and-roll friends in the middle of the woods?" I said. "No. Only you."

The ranger had left an enormous mound of luggage at the signpost for Treble Cliff. The three of us grabbed our stuff. If climbing the hill had been hard the first time, dragging our luggage with us could've been an Olympic event. I was dying to rinse off, and the hike to the shower house, wherever it was, would've been totally worth it.

By the time we got back to our tent, we had our last bunkmate. This girl was tiny, her curly black hair cut super, super short. The only big things about her were her wide-set eyes and her smile, which flashed dazzling white against her dark brown skin. She threw her arms around Shauna's waist, which was basically as high as she could reach, and Shauna returned the hug.

"Hi," the new girl said, turning to Olivia and me and sticking out her hand. "Toni Davis, at your service." Her grip was knuckle crunching.

"Toni and I have been camp friends for years," Shauna said, her arm around Toni's shoulders. "Get this: she's a classically trained pianist . . . and rapper."

"Classically trained pianist and rapper," Olivia echoed. "Is that a thing?"

"As sure as a Jewish country singer is," Toni said. She and Shauna slapped hands.

"What about you two?" Shauna asked. "What's your jam?"

"Oh, Melly and I are up for almost anything," Olivia said. "We've been getting into the classics lately. You know, the Who, the Stones, that kind of thing. Anything, so long as it rocks."

The way she said it made us sound cooler than we were. At least at our school, it wasn't enough to rock out in your basement. Until you'd played your first block party, you were just one more kind of nerd. If obsessing over music gave us any more cred than playing video games or competing in spelling bees, I had yet to notice. But it was fun.

I think Shauna was waiting for me to say something,

too. But since Olivia had already answered for both of us, I only shrugged in agreement.

The four of us teamed up to hang our mosquito netting. Shauna and Toni were experts. When we were finished, it looked like we each had a green gauze cage suspended over our beds.

"Hey, weird question," Olivia said as we rolled out our sleeping bags. "Where are all the boys? Did they get abducted by aliens on their way from auditions?"

Toni and Shauna burst out laughing. "I wish!" Toni said.

"Their units are on the other side of camp," Shauna explained. "Trust me, you'll see plenty of them at practice, meals, activities. It's actually really nice to get a break from them."

I was just as glad. Not that I had anything in particular against boys, but I'd seen too many movies where boys sneaked into girls' slumber parties to steal their underwear. Plus, I didn't want to risk boys seeing me wearing my pajamas with no bra underneath. It was bad enough that our bathroom was so far away. Bathrooms were supposed to be down the hall, not down a hill.

"Why?" Toni asked. "Are you looking for *loooooove?*"

"Of course not!" Olivia said. "I'm here to play music, like everybody else."

We all turned at a knock on our tent pole. A head of blue hair popped inside. "All set?" Blair asked. "We're meeting in the fire circle in two minutes."

"We'll be right out," Shauna said. "Ready, sisters?"

She reached out and linked elbows with Toni, who linked elbows with Olivia, who linked elbows with me, and suddenly I was being towed out of our tent into the pine-scented sunshine. I'd never had a sister before—never even had someone call me sister. But even though I'd known Shauna and Toni less than half an hour, it didn't feel as weird as I would've expected.

four

The afternoon was total information overload. Poppy and Blair led us in a name game. We each had to make up a jingle to help everyone remember our names. Let's just say when your name only rhymes with jiggly words like *belly* and *jelly*, it's bad news.

The rules came next, about bedtime and wake-up time, about keeping our tents clean. Not feeding woodland creatures, not flushing nonflushable items down the toilets, not climbing trees, not setting things on fire except in the fire circle under adult supervision. I started to wonder what catastrophes had prompted someone to write these things down. It all seemed like common sense. But maybe common sense isn't all that common.

Finally it was time to go to the lodge for dinner. Instead of going straight there, though, we stopped in a clearing dominated by a wooden sculpture shaped like a giant electric guitar. The guitar's white body was marked *Unit*. The colorful neck, where the frets and tuners of a real guitar would be, was labeled with different locations: lodge, library, lake, and so on. The entire thing was covered with little hooks.

Olivia and I had passed it earlier, on our way to Treble Cliff, but I hadn't thought too hard about it. I figured it was somebody's bizarre choice of lawn ornament. Maybe the director with the bad handwriting and the bad puns, Damon.

"Welcome to the Fretboard," Poppy said. "As you've probably gathered, Camp Rockaway divides up campers by age. Treble Cliff is the junior high girls' unit, but we've also got units for high school and younger girls. Same goes for the boys."

Blair jumped in. "The younger kids do most of their activities with their units, but you've got a lot more freedom. There are certain times you're expected to be certain places, like meals, lights-out, or band practice. Beyond that, it's up to you. You want to shoot hoops? Knock yourself out. You want to get in some extra practice in the stalls? Go for it. But with great power comes great responsibility, am I right?"

"We've got some Rockaway veterans here," Poppy said. "Who can explain to our newcomers how the Fretboard works?"

I was sure Shauna would volunteer, because she

seemed to know something about everything, but instead Taxi Girl stepped forward. I felt stupid for not remembering her real name from the game. Allison? Annabelle? There were only twelve of us girls in Treble Cliff, plus Poppy and Blair. It should've been easy. But it was lost in the flurry of everything I'd been trying to absorb.

"Thanks, Adeline," Poppy said.

That's right: *Don't call me Madeline, I'm way too gladeline, just call me Adeline!* Her smile, twinkling with braces, seemed to prove it.

"Okay," she said in a loud, clear voice, "you're all going to get a guitar pick with your name on it. It's got a hole drilled in it so you can hang it on the board."

Poppy fished in her pocket and pulled out a handful of picks. "Our picks are yellow," she said. "The other units have other colors to set them apart." She gave me one with my name written in extra-fine-point Sharpie.

"So, I've got my pick," Blair said. "How do I decide where to hang it?"

"If you're with your unit, you can leave it on the body of the guitar, where it says 'Unit.' That's home base," Adeline said. "But if you're doing your own thing, you need to flip your pick to the right place along the neck. That way if someone needs to track you down for any reason, they'll know where to look."

"And we call this monstrosity the Fretboard, why?" Blair asked.

Adeline's grin widened. "So you don't fret about where we are."

Olivia said, "And because Camp Rockaway never, ever walks away from a terrible joke."

"You're catching on already," Blair said proudly. "Go hang up your picks."

Dinner was hot dogs on the lawn outside the lodge, with all the usual things you eat with hot dogs: potato chips, pasta salad, watermelon, chocolate chip cookies. Adeline was ahead of me in line. I noticed her taking her hot dog from a separate, smaller tray. When I got up there, I saw the tray was marked *Veggie*. Apparently vegetarianism went along with being into peace and love and killing fascists.

I took a regular hot dog, feeling a little guilty, and then feeling silly for feeling guilty. I'd never felt guilty about eating meat before. Was I afraid of what Adeline thought? Why should I care, anyway?

I sat in a sunny spot with Olivia, Toni, and Shauna. It seemed like most people were sticking with their bunkmates. As we munched our hot dogs, Olivia asked, "So, when do we get our band assignments?"

"Right after breakfast tomorrow," Toni said.

Olivia groaned. "I don't think I can wait that long."

Shauna said, "The teachers get together tonight and compare notes."

"How do they choose who goes with who?" Olivia asked, shifting closer to me. Not that we had any reason to be worried. We'd put on our applications that we were coming to camp together. As long as we had each other, it didn't matter who else we were put with.

"Partly by instrument, of course," said Shauna. "Like, each band gets a drummer."

"Except there's always too many guitar players," Toni said. "That's just a fact of life."

"Tell me about it," Shauna said. "Oh, and there's always some random violinists or accordion players. They get sprinkled in at the end."

"Accordion players?" Olivia said.

"It happens!"

"It's also by your type of music," Toni said. "Like, if I'm into Beyoncé, they won't stick me with a bunch of Beach Boys wannabes."

"Basically, band assignments determine your future at camp," Shauna said. "Whoever you end up with, you're going to spend a lot of time with them. Which can totally rule or totally suck, depending."

"What about how good you are?" I asked, nibbling nervously on my watermelon rind. "What if they put you in a band and you, um, you can't keep up?"

Shauna and Toni looked at each other, obviously thinking, *Uh-oh, don't put me in a band with Melly.*

But Toni said, "I wouldn't worry about that. Damon

tries really hard to keep Camp Rockaway—what's the word he uses, Shauna?"

"Cooperative, not competitive," Shauna said. "It's true, Melly. The prodigies are up the road at Interlochen. There's a lot of talent here, but it's more about having a good time than anything else, you know?"

"Right," Toni said. "The music stuff's great, but let's be real, I can form a band anywhere. But I can't see the stars at home in the Detroit 'burbs. I can't canoe on a lake. I can't make s'mores over a campfire." Her eyes shone.

Olivia told Toni, "You ought to do ads for this place."

She flashed her enormous grin. "Why, thank you. I've often thought if music doesn't work out, I'll go into marketing."

As dinner wound down, Damon stood on a folding chair outside the door of the lodge. He looked a little younger than my parents, with thinning strawberry blond hair and a big beard. Tiny round glasses glinted over his pink cheeks. His Camp Rockaway T-shirt strained against his belly. He could be Santa Claus in another fifty years.

"Good evening, rock stars!" he bellowed. "Did you enjoy your meal?"

An earsplitting, rock-concert-quality cheer, complete with hooting and whistling, rose from the lawn. If anyone hated hot dogs, they weren't going to spoil the mood by admitting it.

"Fantastic. We've got a real treat for your first night at camp. Your staff is going to be working you hard the next couple of weeks, pushing you to your musical limits. But if you've played in a band before, you know it's not just about playing your instrument well. It's about working together. It's about give and take. That stuff isn't easy, and we know it."

Damon paused and pushed his glasses up his nose.

"That's why tonight we're giving you a demonstration of our skills, so you can see we're not talking out of our behinds. All of your staff are terrific musicians on their own, yet many of them met each other for the first time this summer. You'll get a sense of what can be accomplished in a short time if you go into this experience with dedication and an open mind. And, of course, we hope you'll have a blast. Thank you, and welcome to Camp Rockaway."

Damon stepped down from his chair. Counselors began weaving among the campers, telling us to finish up and herding us into the lodge. The four of us stood and threw away our trash.

The lodge was a large building with stone walls and exposed wooden beams. Inside, all the dining tables and chairs had been folded up and pushed aside to clear space in front of a stage, a real one, wired up with lights and mics and amps and cables coiled neatly on the floor. I counted a drum set, a keyboard, and several guitars—electric, acoustic, bass—in stands. A saxophone, a trumpet. A banjo, a mandolin. I lost track.

The musicians took the stage. Damon sat behind the drums—I don't know why that surprised me, but it kind of did—and Poppy stepped behind the keyboard. My breath caught as the counselor who'd auditioned me, Donna, pulled the strap of an electric guitar over her head. And there were half a dozen more. By the time they'd all taken their places, the stage was packed. The houselights dimmed, Damon clicked his sticks together, and the bright, joyful intro to "Walking on Sunshine" blasted through large black speakers.

They were good. Like, really good.

Nobody needed an invitation to dance. Well, I sort of bounced nervously. But the crowd was so thick, boys and girls, little kids and teenagers and counselors all mixed together, it didn't really matter. A dopey smile hung off my face. Here we were, miles from the nearest gas station, the nearest grocery store, the nearest school or mall or anything at all—in the midst of a live rock show.

"You know why they do this, right?" Shauna shouted as she whirled by.

"Damon said it's to prove the counselors practice what they preach," Olivia yelled back.

"That's the official line. But really it's to wear us out so we sleep tonight!"

It was working. Looking back at the day, it was hard to believe that just this morning Mom had informed me Dad was staying in Kalamazoo to hunt for an apartment instead of driving me to camp. I was suddenly exhausted, and a little bit queasy. It was weird. Part of me wanted to obsess over the trouble at home. Part of me wanted to be miserable, to pick at the wound so it wouldn't have a prayer of scabbing over. And the tireder I got, the bigger that part of me grew and the harder I had to fight it.

I was relieved when the music finally ended and the lights came back up. Olivia and I gathered around Poppy and Blair with the other girls from our unit and began the hike back to Treble Cliff. Darkness hadn't yet fallen, but everything had turned smudgy. Smudgy trees, smudgy sky, the color sucked out of the scenery until nothing was left but shades of gray. Our group bustled with leftover excitement, but the farther we walked into the woods, the quieter we got—as if the gently blowing leaves were telling us *shhh, shhh,* and we were listening.

The buzz and hum of the afternoon had gone, but

still my ears rang. I thought at first it was from the show, which had been loud enough that Mom would've run for her Excedrin, but no. It was different: chirping, trilling. I fell behind the rest of the group as I peered into the trees, searching for the source.

"It's the frogs," someone said.

I jumped—speaking of frogs—and felt ridiculous. It was Taxi Girl. Adeline.

"Tree frogs and tree toads," she said. "And peepers, down by the lake. There's crickets in there, too, probably. But mostly the frogs drown out everything else."

"I thought frogs said *ribbit*," I said.

"That's just the Hollywood frog."

When I laughed, Adeline said, "I'm serious! I mean, it's really the Pacific tree frog. But that's what you always hear in the movies, because it lives right in Hollywood. Now everyone thinks all frogs say *ribbit*—in America, anyway."

"What do frogs say in other countries?" I asked.

"I have no idea. I'm still trying to learn what all the American frogs say." She laughed. "I love the tree toads especially. Have you ever taken a stick and run it along a picket fence? That's what their call reminds me of."

I listened hard, trying to pick out the sound of the tree toads from the rest.

"It's like when you listen to a song for the first time,

and everything sounds like a jumble," Adeline said. "But the more you listen to it, the more you can pick out the different instruments, the harmonies."

"It's different from what I'm used to," I said. "Back home, you hear cicadas and traffic and kids playing in the street. Sometimes a train."

"It's just a different song," Adeline said. "Trust me, you'll fall in love with it."

I was pretty sure it was already happening.

"Hey! Melly!" Olivia had stopped on the path ahead. "You're going to get lost if you don't stick with the group. And I heard a rumor there are bears in these woods."

I called back, "It's okay, I'm with—" But Adeline was already jogging past Olivia to catch up with the others. Her white shirt faded in the deepening darkness.

"Everything okay?" Olivia asked, her eyebrows drawn together.

"Of course," I said. "Adeline and I were just talking about—"

I stopped. The next word should've been *frogs,* of course, but I didn't want to say it. Maybe because it sounded stupid, and I didn't want to remember the conversation that way. It was just a couple of minutes long, but it felt like a big deal. Most people don't go out of their way to talk to shy people. Besides Olivia, I didn't have many other friends, and those I did have I'd made slowly. Today had been a revolution—first Shauna, then Toni, and now Adeline, who was friendly and funny and knew things about frogs. I didn't want to risk spoiling that memory.

So instead I said, "The show."

"Oh," said Olivia. In her voice, I could hear the words she didn't say: *Is that really all?*

"Come on," I said, taking her hand and pulling her along. "We don't want to get left behind, do we? I hear there are bears in these woods."

five

The tension at breakfast was as thick as the sticky gray oatmeal lumped in our bowls. Everyone was speculating about band assignments—counting up the different types of musicians in each age group and comparing favorite artists. But nobody could know for sure until the names were read.

It occurred to me they made Monday oatmeal day for a reason. Everyone actually ate it in hopes of getting to the announcements faster.

Finally the tables were cleared and wiped, and Damon took the stage with one of Camp Rockaway's endless supply of clipboards. "Good morning, rock stars," he said, his voice carrying through the lodge without the need for a mic. It helped that we were completely silent, waiting breathlessly. "The moment you've been waiting for: band assignments!"

He began with the youngest campers. "Because

they have the shortest attention spans," Shauna said. The room rippled with excitement as they learned who they'd be playing with and which instructor they'd be working with.

Then Damon moved on to our group, and Olivia gripped my hand so hard my knuckles ground together. "This is it, Melly," she said.

Toni was assigned to the first group, in Uluru. Shauna was put in Zuma. Then Damon said, "With Chad, in Gibraltar, at ten thirty. From Bass Cliff, Bret and Noel. From Treble Cliff, Olivia and Candace."

Not Melly. Candace. I couldn't remember a face—or even a jingle—to go with the name, but when I looked around the hall, it was obvious she was the tall girl with wavy chestnut hair, beaming. Olivia didn't let go, but her hand went slack around mine. My stomach curdled.

"No," Olivia said. "That can't be right."

Damon kept reading names, filling up Plymouth and Guatapé without mentioning my name. Then finally, "With Donna, in Trolltunga, at ten thirty. From Bass Cliff, David and Caleb. From Treble Cliff, Adeline and Melissa."

He moved on to the oldest campers, leaving Olivia and me stunned.

We were a team. A rhythm section. We had a whole system of communication—different nods and eyebrow wiggles. Olivia was the only bassist I'd ever played with, and the thought of working with someone new scared me. I'd screw up everything. After my lousy audition, Donna must be regretting that she'd ended up with me. I was going to make her even sorrier.

As soon as Damon stepped down from the stage, the lodge exploded into movement and noise. Olivia pulled me up from the table. "I can't believe they didn't put us together!" she said, dragging me across the room. "We've got to talk to Damon before this goes any further."

Olivia planted us in front of Damon, where he sat sorting his stack of papers. His eyebrows went up. "Girls. What can I do for you?"

"There's been a mistake," Olivia said. "Melly and I came to camp together. We're supposed to be in the same band."

Damon looked from Olivia to me and back again. He didn't say anything. I couldn't tell what he was thinking behind his beard.

"Check our applications if you don't believe me. It's right on there," she said. "See, Melly plays drums, and I play bass. We've been playing together for years. We're *tight*."

"That's terrific," he said. "There's nothing like a great musical partnership."

Olivia brightened. "So, you'll do a little switcheroo and fix things?"

Damon shook his head. "Part of the Camp Rockaway experience is to learn to play with new people. Embrace it as part of the challenge."

"But it's on our applications." Olivia's voice grew a hard edge—an edge that sounded mean, but I knew from experience meant she was close to tears.

Olivia wasn't used to hearing no. I don't mean she was spoiled, exactly, just that she had good ideas, so people usually came around to her way of thinking. Like me going to the instrument petting zoo, and Ms. Estrada letting her play electric guitar. Olivia denied it, but I was pretty sure she was the one who'd finally convinced my parents I needed a drum set. Otherwise my percussion career might have been confined to the back row of the music room forever.

But Damon didn't budge. "I hear what you're saying," he said. "You girls will have plenty of chances to be together. Meals, time in your unit, your other camp activities. But this is one area you'll need to be self-reliant. I know it's scary—"

Olivia bristled and stood a little taller.

"—but you can do it. And I believe you'll come out stronger people and musicians at the end. I've been doing this for fifteen years. Trust me. Now, go and have a great day." Damon stood and waved good-bye. We had no choice but to walk away.

"Ugh, this is stupid," Olivia said as we hiked back to Treble Cliff. "It's like school, where they always try to split friends up into different classrooms or project groups. They say it's to make you grow as a person or whatever, but if you ask me, it's a total power trip."

I nodded.

"Damon wouldn't even have known we were friends if we hadn't asked to be put together! We should've pretended not to know each other. We should've come up in separate cars. Set up in different tents."

"It'll be okay," I said.

"No, it won't. I screwed up everything."

"There was no way you could know."

"But I promised you. You were anxious about coming here, and I said, 'It'll be okay, we'll be together,' and now we're not going to be together."

"Just during band practice," I said, uncomfortable. It was one thing when my parents called me Mouse. It was another when my best friend treated me like one. Besides, if anyone was acting anxious, it was Olivia. I wasn't the biggest fan of surprises, but after my parents' news, Damon's pronouncement didn't seem like that big an issue.

"You don't need to worry about me," I said. "I'd rather play with you, of course. But I'll deal. We'll both deal."

"I guess we don't have much choice in the matter," Olivia said. "It's a long walk home."

We ambled in silence. The tension dissolved in the warm air.

"So," I said, "Candace. I can't remember what she plays."

Olivia snorted. "She's one of those random violin players Shauna warned us about. And don't think I can't tell you're changing the subject. If you're trying to make me not mad at Damon, it won't work."

I smiled. "You can be mad to your heart's content. I won't stop you."

"And you're with Gladeline. I bet you'll end up playing happy hippie music."

So Olivia had noticed the "Peace Love Music" sticker, too. "Maybe," I said. "Or maybe I'll introduce her to metal. Teach her to embrace her inner Madeline."

Maybe that was another reason I wasn't feeling too bad about my band assignment. Sure, it was disappointing not to be with Olivia, and I was more scared of Donna than I cared to admit. But I was also excited to spend more time with Adeline. I *did* want to know what kind of music she liked. I wanted to know how she knew about frogs, and whether she was always a vegetarian, and why she came to camp in a taxi. I wanted to know how guitars could kill fascists. It seemed like playing in a band with her would be a good way to get answers.

But telling Olivia this stuff wouldn't make her feel any better.

"Oh, Melly." She groaned. "I know Damon's right, and we'll be together almost all the time. But being in different bands? It's like being on different teams. It's like being from different countries. Different planets."

"Wow," I said. "Maybe we should've signed up for drama camp instead."

Pouting, Olivia shoved my shoulder. I stumbled off the path into a tree. I was fine, just a little dizzy, but Olivia ran to my side and put her arm around my shoulders. "Oh my God, Melly! Are you okay? Did you hurt something? Your ankle? I'm such an idiot. Here, lean on me."

"'When you're not strong,'" I sang, and did a little chorus girl kick.

I knew she would recognize the song. It was in Grandma Goodwin's collection of old 45s, and on a visit last winter Olivia and I had played it so many times it was a miracle the needle didn't dig grooves clear through the vinyl. It was also a miracle Grandma didn't go insane listening to us, but she just smiled and said it was one of her favorites. Olivia said it was our song. The perfect song for best friends forever.

Olivia let go, and I tripped all over again. "You goof,"

she said. "You're not hurt!"

"What? You won't be my friend? You won't help me carry on?" I giggled.

"I can't believe you fool people into thinking you're a shrinking little violet."

"What can I say?" I said, skipping ahead. "You're the only one who knows the real me."

The oldest campers had band practice first, giving us over an hour to kill. Shauna advised us to visit the shower house. "The little kids are at the beach and stuff with their units in the morning, so it's the perfect time for us to get in there," she said. "No line!"

I expected the showers to be like the ones at the Y, just a bunch of spigots in a wide-open tiled room. I hated showering at the Y. It didn't matter how many times my mother said, "We're all girls here. There's nothing to be embarrassed about." She was probably trying to convince herself as much as me. She wouldn't even walk around the house without a robe to cover her pajamas, and that was with just Dad and me.

Emphasis on *was*.

It turned out the showers at Camp Rockaway were totally different. The best, most important thing was they had individual stalls with curtains. The strangest, coolest thing was they had no ceilings. Everything was open-air. If you looked up, there were the leaves of the trees, and the blue sky beyond. If it were raining, you'd get rained on—but that hardly mattered, since getting wet was the whole point!

In fact, when I pulled the shower chain, the spray felt like warm, gentle rain against my skin. I closed my eyes and breathed in deep. Rain on my shoulders and sunshine on my face, I imagined staying at camp forever: sneaking into the practice cabins to sleep at night, stealing food from the lodge, showering under the sun. It didn't sound too bad.

A sharp sting jarred me. I slapped at my leg, leaving a mutilated mosquito and a smear of blood for me to scrub off.

At ten thirty, we were back in the clearing with the practice cabins. Olivia had retrieved her bass from her locker. I had my sticks. We both had our water bottles, filled to the brim and still icy from one of Camp Rockaway's woodland wells.

Outside Gibraltar, Olivia said, "I regret to inform you that, thanks to a certain bearded camp director who shall not be named, I must leave you now. However, I'll be back to rescue you in ninety minutes. Hang in there, okay?"

"Somehow I think I'll survive," I said.

Adeline was already outside Trolltunga, waiting for the previous group to come out. She was wearing a Marquette Food Co-op T-shirt, cut-off corduroy pants, and hemp sandals. Olivia's happy hippie assessment was probably not far off the mark. Her face lit up when she saw me. "Melly! Yay, bandmates!"

I smiled back and echoed, "Yay, bandmates."

"Do you realize in all my summers at camp, I've never been in a band with a girl drummer?" Adeline said. "This is awesome. You're awesome."

"Oh," I said. I was pretty sure being a girl didn't affect my ability. And while female drummers were in the minority in the rock world, I hadn't chosen drums to make a political statement. I wondered what Shauna would say. She'd have the appropriate feminist response.

Instead, I stuck to the obvious. The *extremely* obvious. "You play acoustic?"

"Yeah, I guess I'm kind of old-school," Adeline said. "Anyway, it does the job."

I didn't have a chance to ask what she meant, because just then our remaining bandmates walked up. The first boy had a chalky complexion and spiky blond hair that wasn't much darker. He wore all black. The other boy had light brown skin and black hair flopping over his eyes, so I could barely see his face. He wore a shirt that said Wyoming Junior High. I smiled to think of one junior high serving the entire state of Wyoming, until I realized Wyoming was probably the name of a town. Then I was really glad I hadn't said anything. Sometimes being shy pays.

"Hey," Adeline said. "What's up?"

The blond boy grunted. The black-haired boy stared at the ground. *This will go well—not.*

The cabin door swung open. A bunch of high schoolers trooped out, and Donna gestured for us to come inside. Today her inky hair was pulled into a high ponytail, choppy strands escaping the elastic. She wore a T-shirt with a unicorn skeleton on it, cut off at the sleeves and waist. She also wore cargo pants cut off at the knees and scuffed combat boots. In other words, she looked every inch a rock star.

She must have thought I was such a poseur.

Now that I wasn't paralyzed with fear over my audition, I looked around the cabin. The floor was covered with rugs. The walls and ceiling were lined with rippled foam. Besides the drums, the room was equipped with a full-length keyboard, cables and amps, mics, and music stands. A chalkboard hung on the wall across from the drums. A portable stereo sat on a shelf.

Donna shut the door. Instantly the temperature seemed to rise ten degrees. Without windows, Trolltunga was practically a sauna. "Have a seat, everyone," Donna said.

This time I went straight for the stool behind the

drums. Donna surveyed us through half-shut eyes, her mouth a straight line. "All right," she said. "Let's get introduced. Name, instrument, and how long you've been playing. Let's start with our drummer."

I itched under my bandmates' gaze as I said, "Melly, drums, almost three years."

Then came Adeline. "Adeline, acoustic guitar, five years."

The floppy-haired boy was next. He mumbled, "David, bass, two years."

Last came the blond boy. "I'm Caleb," he said. "I've been playing since I was six, and I'm here to play metal. Last year I got stuck in a band full of Radio Disney freaks, and I lost a piece of my soul that I'll never get back."

"Noted," Donna said coolly. "This might be a good time to talk about expectations. I'm sure you have your own, and we'll have plenty of opportunities to address those. But for now, let's talk about *my* expectations. Honestly, I don't care how long you've been playing. I don't care what kind of music you like. The moment you walk in that door each day, you are all on equal footing. Everyone deserves their fellow musicians' respect."

She held each of our gazes in turn until we nodded.

"Camp Rockaway has whole sessions devoted to teaching rookies their instruments. Since you're not at one of them, I'm assuming you already know how to play. But if you ever get stuck, I can step in and help. More than anything, you are here to learn how to be a band. I am the training wheels keeping you upright as you find your balance. The goal is that by the end of camp, we can take off the training wheels, and you will ride on your own. Sound good?"

We all nodded.

"Let me hear you say it," Donna said.

"Sounds good," Adeline said. The rest of us murmured our agreement.

"Okay," said Donna, "yesterday at your auditions you had the opportunity to express your musical preferences. I've taken the liberty of choosing four songs, each with one of you in mind. We're going to tackle them over the next few days, one at a time. From that point on, if there's something else you want to play, it's up to you to let me know."

She grabbed four folders from the floor and passed them out. I opened mine to find a Camp Rockaway pencil and a single chart with "I Knew You Were Trouble" written at the top.

"Taylor Swift?" Caleb said, horrified. "This is the total opposite of my preference!"

"Really?" Donna said. "I must have been thinking of someone else when I picked it."

Caleb shot Adeline a dirty look. I wasn't sure how he'd decided it was her fault, but I felt relief. I liked

Taylor Swift. Her songs were so catchy that whenever they came on the radio, in the car or at the store, I couldn't help tapping along to the beat. The only reason I'd never played her songs on drums was Olivia had deemed her music too poppy. Still, I didn't want to get on Caleb's bad side. I didn't want to get on anyone's bad side.

Adeline smiled brightly. "Looks like it's not your day, Caleb."

Caleb's skin went from white to purple. "Freaking chick music," he muttered.

Donna, who'd been slouching against the chalkboard, was upright in a flash. "Excuse me?" she said. "In this room, there is no 'chick music.' There is no 'dude music' or 'bro music.' There is music. Period. There are different musical genres. There are male and female musical artists. But music is music. Is that understood?"

Everyone nodded, even Caleb.

"Let me hear you say it: music is music."

"Music is music," we repeated.

Donna nodded. "And now, ready or not, we are going to make some."

Donna was one of the strictest teachers I'd ever had—and we hadn't even begun playing.

Six

Practice was, to put it nicely, rocky.

Things started out okay. "First we'll just listen," Donna said. "Don't worry about the lyrics or chords. Just soak up the music. Feel it in your body. If it helps, close your eyes."

She pushed play on the stereo, and the short, bright opening chords of "I Knew You Were Trouble" burst from the speakers. The song was pretty straightforward: four-four time, medium tempo, basic chord progression, simple lyrics. It was guitar heavy, too, which was probably good considering Caleb and Adeline were the most experienced players. Plus, I was sure everyone—including Caleb, even if he despised it—had heard it plenty of times before. I didn't know what other songs Donna had up her sleeve, but it made sense to start with this one.

The only confusing thing was the lyrics. I'd never

thought too hard about them before, but now that I was staring at the chart I couldn't help it. If you knew someone was trouble when they walked in, why would you want to get involved with them? Why would you doom yourself to misery and failure? Come to think of it, probably 95 percent of rock songs were about unhealthy relationships. Maybe it simply reflected reality. I mean, I never thought my parents' relationship was unhealthy, and now they were splitting up, so what did I know?

At the end, Donna said, "I'm going to play it again. And this time I want you to sing."

Wait a minute—this wasn't part of the deal! I'd come to camp to play drums, not to show the world just how lacking I was in the vocal department. David must have felt the same way. He looked up, his eyes wide and alarmed.

"Singing together is one of the surest ways to not only learn a song but also stay in sync," Donna said. "At least, that's my opinion, and as the teacher, my opinion goes."

"I'm not a very good singer," I said in a low voice. David nodded vigorously.

"It's rock and roll, for crying out loud," Donna said. "Taylor Swift's talent is mostly in her attitude, not her vocal cords. Anyway, it's just us here. Sing." She requeued the music.

We were mostly terrible. Caleb's voice kept cracking.

David barely mouthed the words. I sang only slightly louder, because even though I knew the melody by heart, I kept missing notes.

Only Adeline seemed comfortable. She sat at the edge of her chair, shoulders relaxed, head tipped back a little as if she were singing to the clouds and the ceiling just happened to get in the way. Her voice wouldn't blow anyone away with its power. It was a little bit rough, a little bit sweet. But it was full of feeling. It was real.

I was flooded with a mixture of admiration and envy. I hoped she'd rub off on the rest of us before the end-of-camp concert.

The third time through, Donna finally let us play our instruments. "Take it slow," she said, picking up her acoustic. "Keep it simple, as simple as you can. Rome was not built in a day, yada yada yada. Oh, and don't forget to sing."

You might think with Donna leading us we'd be okay. Not great, but not disastrous either. Nope. David and I couldn't get in sync. Every time I looked his way, he was doing his own thing, just a little bit off from me. I couldn't catch his eye because his hair was in the way. But it probably didn't matter, because I don't think Caleb was even listening to us. He was what Ms. Estrada called "off to the races," like faster meant better. But I had no room to talk. If I'd thought my audition was bad, this was twenty times worse. I was so nervous

I dropped a stick. And forget the singing!

We only made it through the first verse before Donna stopped us. She exhaled, aiming a jet of air at her bangs, but they were plastered to her forehead. "Five-minute break," she said, grabbing her water bottle and taking a swig. "Hydrate. Stretch. Come back ready to try again."

Heading outside with my own water bottle, I checked my watch. I couldn't believe practice was only half over. I felt worn out, mentally and physically, like I'd just completed some horrible combination of oral report and cross-country run.

Make that half completed—ugh.

"Hanging in?" Adeline said.

"Um, yeah. I think I'll survive. Probably." It was funny, but the second Adeline started talking to me, I didn't feel so tired anymore. "Is it always like this?"

"Which part of it?" Adeline asked. "Working so hard? Or worrying we'll suck forever?"

"Both," I said, and laughed because she'd read my mind.

She grinned. "It's always work, although I will say"—she lowered her voice—"Donna's tougher than most of the teachers I've had." She shrugged. "Starting out with a new group is always hard, though. We'll get better."

"I hope so," I said, "or I may never be able to show

my face at Camp Rockaway again."

"Now, that would be a tragedy," Adeline said. "Want to practice with me this afternoon? I figured I'd do that for a while, then hang out at the lake."

"Oh! Maybe," I said. "I should probably ask Olivia first, though. She was bummed out about our band assignments. We came here together, and it was kind of a shock when Damon split us up."

"She could come, too," Adeline said. "It's cool to see what other bands are playing."

"That would be great." I hesitated. Olivia had been blowing off steam when she called Adeline a hippie. Still, she hadn't said it in a very nice way. I added, "But I'll have to ask her."

Adeline nodded. "Sure. Just let me know."

I thought maybe the hardest part of our morning practice was over. Donna interrupted the song frequently to walk us through transitions, make us try a measure again when we flubbed it, and point out details from the recording that hadn't made it onto our charts. But as time went on, Caleb's fingers got faster and sloppier. David seemed to shrink into himself, his bass mumbling as much as he did. It was all I could do to hold down the beat.

At least Adeline kept her cool. Maybe it was because she'd come to Camp Rockaway before. Maybe it was because she was Gladeline. Whatever. I'd take it.

Donna's watch beeped at noon. We'd finally—barely—made it through the entire song.

"Not bad, people," she said, but it sounded like she was saying it out of habit, not because she believed it. "I want you to run through it some more in your free time."

I swallowed a groan. At this point, I never wanted to hear it—much less play it—again.

Donna continued. "Respect your bandmates by coming to practice prepared. Remember, we're all in this together. Caleb, Adeline, stay behind a minute. There are a couple of things I want you to focus on as you work independently."

David left ahead of me and quickly loped toward the lodge for lunch. I'd only taken a few steps before Olivia pounced on me. "So, how'd it go?" she asked.

"Well . . ." I tried to figure out how to put the best spin on things. "It was our first time playing together."

"That bad, huh?"

"Let's just say there's plenty of room for improvement," I said. "How about you?"

Olivia sighed. "Considering you weren't there, I guess it was okay. I asked Candace how long she'd been playing violin, and you know what she said? Since she was three. Three! Why isn't she at Interlochen? Or in a country band with Shauna, fiddling till the cows come home? And the drummer, Bret? He said, 'Call me Brick.'

How pretentious is that? It's like he thinks he's already famous enough to have just one name, like Flea, or Moby, or—"

"Madonna?"

"Yes! Admittedly, he's shaped like a brick. Still, there's no excuse."

"What about the last guy?" I asked.

"Oh," Olivia said in a very different voice. Quiet. Careful. "That's Noel."

"And?"

She gazed at the treetops. "He's a really talented acoustic guitarist. And he's got a good voice."

"And?"

She sighed. "And he's got this dark brown hair that kind of curls over his ears. And these melty brown eyes."

"Uh-huh."

"Plus, afterward, he said I was one of the best bass players he's ever worked with."

I wasn't too stupid to know where this was going. I'd had a crush on a boy named Arjit, a fellow percussionist, for most of seventh grade. He always made snarky comments about the music we were playing. It didn't matter how many times he called John Philip Sousa "John Philip Snooze-a"—I laughed. Sometimes he juggled his sticks. Since we were in the back row, we got away with a lot, and since we paid attention when it counted, the most Ms. Estrada would ever do was shoot us a look if we got too boisterous.

But that was as far as things went. We didn't hang out together outside of band, not even at lunch. We had other classes together, but if we weren't playing drums, we basically ignored each other. Sometimes I imagined what it would be like to kiss Arjit. If I'd had the chance and didn't completely chicken out, I'd have probably done it. I liked him better than any other boy. But I wasn't about to break down the door separating me from the kids with boyfriends and girlfriends.

Olivia, on the other hand? Total door breaker.

She'd never had a boyfriend, either, though she'd gotten her first kiss playing Truth or Dare at Stella's birthday party. But she couldn't wait for it to happen. I'd lost track of how many notes she'd asked me to pass, asking so-and-so to ask so-and-so if so-and-so liked her. How many times she'd texted me before school to say, *HELP! What should I wear?!?!* because there was a chance she'd pass the boy she liked in the hallway. If I'd thought Camp Rockaway would be any different, I'd just been proven wrong.

"There's one problem," Olivia said. "I think Candace likes Noel, too."

Suddenly I smelled drama on the breeze.

Seven

Poppy and Blair told us that by state law we had to
rest quietly for an hour after lunch. And because this
was Camp Rockaway, rest hour wasn't called rest hour.
It was called B-flat.

Get it? Be flat?

The four of us were in bed. Toni lay perfectly still
on her back, her hands clasped over her chest. She
looked like a corpse but insisted she was meditating.
Shauna propped herself on an elbow and wrote in a
spiral-bound notebook. Olivia was engrossed in an
issue of *Bass Player.* Theoretically I was reading *The
Beat of My Own Drum,* a memoir by drumming great
Sheila E. My parents had given it to me for my thir-
teenth birthday back in May. In reality I was struggling
to keep my eyes open.

A knock came on the tent pole. "Mail call," Poppy

announced. "Toni, I've got a couple of letters for you. Olivia, one for you, too."

Olivia rolled her eyes as she reached out from under her mosquito netting for the pink envelope. "I swear, my mom is such a helicopter parent. It's barely been twenty-four hours!"

"And she must have mailed it last Friday for it to get here today," I pointed out.

"Worse," Olivia said, pointing at the postmark. "Wednesday. It probably got here before I even packed my suitcase."

"At least she cares," I said.

I knew it was silly to think my parents didn't care— it was only Monday, for Pete's sake—but given what happened over the weekend I kind of felt like they owed me. On the other hand, what could they have possibly written? *Dear Melly, guess what we're doing this weekend? Ruining your life and sending you hundreds of miles away without another word!*

It was just as well they hadn't. I didn't want to think about them anyway.

Shauna said, "If anyone has helicopter parents, it's Toni. Two letters, already? Sheesh!"

"Ha," Toni said glumly. "Every summer they get the entire family to write me letters. The catch is I've got to write back to every single person. I can kiss meditation good-bye for the rest of camp." She sighed and hung over the side of her bed, digging a pad of paper and a pen out of her suitcase. "Dear Aunt Crystal," she dictated before lapsing into grim silence, her pen scratching across the page.

For some reason, Toni's pouting cheered me up. I lay back, smiling, and actually read a few pages of my book before Blair called that B-flat was over.

"So what's everyone doing this afternoon?" Olivia asked. I suddenly realized I'd forgotten to mention Adeline's invitation to hang out.

"Shauna and I were talking about practicing for a while and then going to the lake," Toni said, tossing aside her letter writing.

Shauna set down her pen, too. "After all, it wouldn't be camp without me getting a massive sunburn."

"I've got sunscreen if you want it," I said.

"Oh, I've got gallons," Shauna said. "But trust the redhead: the only way for me to avoid a sunburn is to walk around with a blanket over my head."

"I think we should sign out a practice stall," Olivia said to me. "This'll be our only chance to play together today. Besides, it'll be fun—just the two of us, like at home. We've got the whole afternoon, and we don't even have to worry about keeping the volume down!"

Just like that, I knew practicing with Adeline wasn't

going to happen, and neither was the lake. Olivia had used the word *fun*, but I could tell it wasn't just fun to her. It was important. She felt bad about the band assignment snafu, and she wanted to make it up to me with some one-on-one time. Even though I was suddenly conscious of the sweat trickling down my neck, of my skin sticking to the shiny fabric of my sleeping bag, I said, "Sounds good to me."

I got up and slung my stick bag over my shoulder. Music folders and water bottles in hand, we hiked to the lodge to get Olivia's bass and sign out a practice stall and an amp, pausing along the way to flip our picks at the Fretboard.

The practice stalls in the lodge basement were tiny, not much bigger than our bathroom at home if you took out the tub. It was a squeeze. The drums took up nearly the entire space. You had to have three or more people to sign up for one of the larger stalls.

The floor was covered with old rugs, and the walls had rippled foam stapled all around—even the ceiling and the back of the door. Music came through the walls from other rooms, but it was muffled, just the bass. The only surface that wasn't covered was a small window facing into the hallway, so whichever counselor was on duty could peek in.

"Here we are," Olivia said, "the rhythm section! Back together and better than ever."

She set up her bass, moved the music stand so we could both sort of see it, and stacked up the charts. Except for "I Knew You Were Trouble," they were all hers. Obviously her teacher didn't buy into the one-song-at-a-time approach. I wasn't sure what she'd said at her audition, but judging by the artists, she'd ended up in a classic rock band: Led Zeppelin, the Rolling Stones, Pat Benatar, Queen. Then it was just like being at home in my basement. The difference was the basement was always chilly, and here it was hot and stuffy.

But after the morning, it was such a relief playing with Olivia. Even though I didn't know the songs very well, I could count on her to keep time with me. My hands relaxed on my sticks, and instead of all my energy draining into the drums, it felt like the drums were pumping energy into me. I sat up straighter. My head started bobbing. Olivia and I grinned at each other.

Still, there came a point when my forearms got tired, my shirt clung to me, my throat dried up, and my butt hurt. Each time Olivia said, "Let's try that again from the top," I groaned inside. My drumming high was over. All I could think about was that lake down the hill, and how Adeline was probably there by now, and Toni and Shauna, messing around and cooling off, while I sweated to death in the lodge.

Finally I said, "Olivia? I'm out of water."

"Oh! Are you thirsty? I think there's a drinking fountain upstairs."

"Actually, I was thinking maybe we could take a break."

"Sure. You want to take five? Ten? I've got to pee, anyway."

"I . . . I was thinking maybe we could stop for the day." I felt bad, but I couldn't lie.

"Oh." Olivia's face drooped. "Are you sure?"

"Yeah. I mean, my arms are getting kind of tired. And it's really hot in here."

To my relief, Olivia shrugged and put on a smile. "You're right. You're absolutely right. Anyway, we worked hard. No one can accuse us of slacking. Should we change into our suits and head to the lake?"

"Ladies and gentlemen, the amazing Olivia Mendoza!" I said. "She plays bass. She reads minds. Is there anything she can't do?"

She laughed, and it was all good.

Under the clear sky, surrounded by tall evergreens, the lake shone royal blue. Camp Rockaway shared the lake with a sheep farm, and I heard their distant bleating. Unlike the non-*ribbiting* frogs, they really did seem to be saying *baa*—with the bass cranked.

As we approached the water's edge, a sign pointed to the boathouse. It said Joan Jetty. Another sign, pointing to the swimming area, said Let It Beach.

"Har, har," said Olivia mildly. We slipped off our shoes and socks and hung our towels on the fence. I wiggled my toes in the sand. It was soft.

The swimming area was bordered by long white docks on either side. The deep end was marked with yellow ropes connecting to a blue raft. Campers splashed in the water, playing Marco Polo. Others played on the raft or lounged on the beach. A few kids were actually building sand castles on the shore. Two lifeguards wearing red swimsuits and white T-shirts paced the docks, keeping an eye on everyone.

Just looking at the water refreshed me. I waded in.

"Ack, it's cold!" Olivia said, dipping in a toe and pulling it right back out again.

It was. I swallowed my shock, loving the way the water sucked at my ankles, then my shins, as I moved deeper. The ground was pebbly under my feet. Tiny fish circled my ankles but zipped away when I dipped my fingers in to catch one. It was so different from the pool at the Y, which had so much chlorine it burned my eyes and nose.

"What are those things?" Olivia said, backing away—right into Adeline.

Adeline caught her elbow and steadied her. "Hey," she said. "You two made it!" She wore an orange swim cap over her braids, and her purple bikini was bone dry. She must have just arrived, too, which made me feel better about having been cooped up at the lodge so long.

"Yeah!" I said, smiling back at her. "You made it, too!"

She laughed, and I turned pink. Of course she'd made it. It had been her plan all along. Why did I say such inane things?

"Hey," Olivia said, not nearly as enthusiastic as I was.

"What were you two looking at?" Adeline asked. I pointed down into the water, and she leaned over to look. "Oh," she said, "minnows. They won't bite. Leeches, on the other hand . . ."

Olivia was alarmed. "Leeches? Like, bloodsuckers? Where?"

"Sorry, that was mean," Adeline said. "There aren't any leeches in here. They like really mucky water."

"This water doesn't exactly look clean," Olivia said. "It's all brown."

"No, actually, the water's so clear you can see the sand. That's what's brown," Adeline explained. "Look, there's your feet."

"It's still cold," Olivia said. She rubbed her arms.

"It helps if you duck in all at once," Adeline said. "You have to keep moving. It's when you stop that you get cold. Come on. Race me to the raft, and I'll prove it to you."

"I don't think so," Olivia said. "I'm going to lay out for a while."

I knew Olivia's real problem wasn't the cold, the minnows, or the possibly dirty water. The real problem was, unlike me, she'd never taken swimming lessons. She'd never admit it, but she could barely dog-paddle. She tugged at my hand, steering us back toward shore. "Come on, Mel," she said. "This is our time to hang out together, remember?"

Out at the raft, kids were jumping and diving and cannonballing, then splashing around the side to climb back up the ladder. Others sat back, talking and warming up before they jumped in to cool off again. They seemed to be having the best time of anyone at the beach.

It was easy to imagine myself with them, wearing my brand-new swimsuit covered in turquoise swirls. It was easy to imagine myself with Adeline—Adeline, who wanted to be my friend even though I was shy and said stupid, obvious things.

But Olivia needed me more. "Next time?" I said to Adeline.

She shrugged. "Sure, if you want." Without waiting for me to say anything else, she plunged into the water.

A few seconds later, she burst back out and swam toward the raft.

Olivia and I got our towels and settled onto the scalding sand. My chin propped in my hands, I watched as Adeline organized the kids on the raft into a game of follow the leader. In my mind, I leaped after them, the delicious water swallowing me up. I paddled below the surface until my lungs were empty, and then I drifted, face up, toward the sun.

It was so tempting to join them—to join her. But I couldn't do that. Olivia was always there for me. I couldn't ditch her for some kids' game with someone I barely knew.

That night was firebowl. After dinner, everyone hiked to the amphitheater. It was nestled in the hills, with rows of log benches set in a semicircle overlooking the lake. The counselors had built a towering log cabin of wood, more like a skyscraper, really. As we took our seats, flames began to lick out between the gaps in the logs. Smoke funneled out the top.

The sun was dipping low in the sky across the lake, low enough that it was in our eyes, like a spotlight, when it shone through the trees. With the firelight behind him, Damon was nothing but a shadow holding a guitar. "Welcome," he shouted, "to the first firebowl of camp!"

Everyone clapped and cheered.

"For everyone who's new to Camp Rockaway, here's the deal. Firebowl isn't about performance. It's about community. We've delved into the instrument library and hauled out pretty much every acoustic guitar, hand drum, tambourine, and kazoo in the place. Everyone is welcome to get up front and help lead a song.

"But I'm not here to talk at you. Let's get started with a song everyone knows. And if you don't, trust me: you will by the time you go home, because this is a firebowl favorite."

About ten counselors joined him in the front. In addition to the guitars and percussion instruments, I saw a mandolin, a banjo, and something too small to see until the counselor lifted it to her mouth and I realized it was a harmonica. As they started singing "Take Me Home, Country Roads," kids around me nodded in recognition and joined in.

At first I only listened. I was flashing back to practice that morning, how I'd felt so nervous when Donna made us sing. Plus, I didn't know the words very well. Plus, I was sitting next to Toni, and wow, that girl had pipes. I'd sound like a rusty hinge compared to her. Nobody needed to hear that.

But I quickly realized no one would hear me anyway. The way the amphitheater cupped the sound, it seemed to come from every direction at once. It was so different from the dead sound of Trolltunga or the practice stall. I began to sing, first softly, then louder, and my chest opened up. My heart swelled with the music.

As the evening wore on, older campers stepped down to the front to help lead a song. Hands traded instruments. I didn't know every song, but I listened, and usually by the end I could join in on the chorus or at least hum along. Without even meaning to, I started patting my knees and tapping my feet in rhythm to the music.

"We should go down there some night," Olivia whispered. "Not tonight, but at the next firebowl. Me on guitar, you on djembe."

I eyed the big, goblet-shaped drum hanging at the waist of one of the counselors. He thumped the skin with his palms and slapped the rim, the drum changing pitch depending on where he hit it. "I've never played a djembe."

"You could learn," she said with a shrug. "There's a percussion workshop tomorrow. I saw it posted in the lodge."

As the sun sank farther, the clouds over the lake began to glow bright pink. The sky at the tree line turned orange, yellow, and purple. I never saw such beautiful sunsets back home. There were too many buildings in the way.

But eventually the colors dripped lower and lower to the horizon. The sky above was washed in purplish blue, then almost black. The fire stood out against the darkening backdrop, but even it began to sink like the sun, the wooden tower crumbling in on itself with showers of sparks every time a chunk fell. Tiny bits of ash floated up in spirals.

The songs grew quieter, slower. The campfire was nothing but a loose pile of charred wood and a few glowing embers like blinking red eyes in the dark. Damon said, "This'll wrap up Camp Rockaway, Unplugged, for tonight," and started playing one last song.

When the final notes faded, it wasn't like the end of a school assembly, where everyone explodes back into whatever random conversations they were having before they had to learn about saying no to drugs or cyberbullying. Everyone stood and filed out of the amphitheater without talking. It was as if the firebowl had cast a spell on us.

It wasn't until we were all on the trail outside that the counselors flipped on their flashlights and started calling. "Carole Kingdom, over here!" "Buddy Hollow, by me!" But even as we hiked back to Treble Cliff, the hush stayed with us.

Lying in bed after lights-out, I sank into the hollow of my cot, the darkness cocooning me. My bunkmates were whispering, rehashing the day, but their voices soon turned into background noise as surely as the peepers and tree toads.

The frogs and toads reminded me of Adeline. When I looked back at my day, it wasn't band practice or fire-bowl or hanging out with Olivia that stood out most. It was watching Adeline swim out to the raft, climbing up, and diving off with a clean splash, again and again.

Like throwing herself headlong into the water was the easiest thing in the world.

eight

Miraculously, Adeline was right: the next day, practice went better. Caleb was happy because our new chart was "Enter Sandman," by Metallica. I was happy because Donna made us run through "I Knew You Were Trouble" only a couple of times before we switched gears. I was more than ready for the change.

"Enter Sandman" was sort of an old song, but it still got played on the radio, at least the hard rock station. It had all the traits of a heavy metal classic: driving drumbeat, wailing guitars, raging vocals. Lyrics-wise, though, it was a lullaby, with phrases like *hush little baby, don't say a word.* Imagine the monster under your bed was your babysitter, rocking you to sleep with his band of bogeymen, and you'll get the idea.

The song was obviously a favorite of Caleb's. The moment we picked up our instruments, he was zipping through the entire lead guitar part, from the catchy opening riff to the spine-chilling solo. That left the rest of us to play catch-up. Adeline, especially, didn't seem sure where an acoustic guitar belonged in the mayhem, but she put on a smile anyway and followed Donna on rhythm guitar. As for David and me? Let's just say I'd be spending a hefty chunk of the afternoon practicing, and so would David, if he knew what was good for him.

Donna didn't interrupt us as much as she had yesterday. Instead she shouted instructions over the music. "Nose out of your instruments!" was one of her favorites, when she thought we were getting too wrapped up in our own playing and needed to check in with the rest of the group. "Listen to yourselves!" was another, when she thought we weren't wrapped up enough. And as always, "Sing, people!"

She also kept saying, "Louder, Melly. Louder!"

Seriously? Nobody—not Ms. Estrada, not Olivia—had ever told me to play louder. That was part of what I loved about drums. I could be loud without trying. I could be *too* loud without trying. I was used to dialing things back so I didn't drown out the other instruments, keeping my hands and feet carefully under control. Now Donna wanted more from me? How was I supposed to give it to her? I didn't think I could!

I pretended I couldn't hear her. Eventually she gave up, shaking her head.

On a scale of one to ten, I probably wouldn't have given us more than a three. But when Donna's watch beeped, she said, "Progress." And even though overall David was still mumbling, I was still stumbling, and Caleb was still rushing, I had to agree.

"See?" Adeline mouthed at me.

"I'll never doubt you again," I whispered back.

"You better not," she said, "or there will be consequences."

I raised my eyebrows. "Yeah? Like what?"

"I don't know," she said. "But I'm sure I can think of some—"

Donna cleared her throat loudly. "If I could trouble you for just a moment longer, I'd like to give you each some things to work on when you practice individually."

I blushed at being called out, but Adeline didn't seem to mind. She winked at me, and my embarrassment dissolved into a grin. I didn't even hear what Donna said next. Honestly, at that moment, I didn't care.

At B-flat, there was still no letter from Mom or Dad. *Relax. It's only Tuesday. The only way a letter could've gotten here so fast is if they overnighted it.*

But as Toni grumbled at the arrival of two more letters, my heart twinged. If they'd really cared, my parents *would* have overnighted me a letter, no matter how much it cost. As soon as the thought crossed my mind, I knew how babyish it was, but I couldn't help it.

Olivia scooted around on her cot so that she could put her face close to mine, only our mosquito netting separating us. "Melly? There's something I need to tell you. I haven't been sure how to say it."

Her words gave me just enough time to get completely confused and worried. The possibilities ranged from *My dad has lymphoma* to *You need better deodorant.*

"Just say it," I whispered back.

"I know you and I were going to play this afternoon, but at practice, Noel asked if I'd jam with him," Olivia said. "I told him he should invite you, too, but he really wants Brick."

"Oh," I said, startled. Was that all? "I guess that's okay."

"Are you sure? Because I could tell him I changed my mind."

"I'm sure," I said, though I was wondering what had happened to Olivia's promise to stick by me through the next two weeks. Yesterday she'd been so insistent we spend the afternoon together. "Does this have anything to do with your C-R-U-S-H?"

"Shhh," Olivia said, glancing across the tent at Shauna and Toni. "I don't need the entire world to know. And no, it's not a crush thing. It's a music thing."

"Sure, sure," I said. "Whatever you say."

I wondered how Noel saw it. Had he asked Olivia to play because he liked her as a bass player, or because he liked her back? Not that it mattered. Either way, I was on my own.

"I doubt it'll be the entire afternoon," Olivia said. "Boys have short attention spans, right? I'll totally make it up to you."

"Olivia," I said in a warning voice. "I told you it was fine."

"Okay, okay. Thanks. I'll shut up now."

She did. And after B-flat, she leaped up and practically sprinted for the lodge. Shanna disappeared a moment later, going who knows where. I sat, wondering what to do next.

Toni was changing into her swimsuit. "Olivia ditched you, huh?"

"That sounds meaner than it was," I said.

"If you say so."

"Anyway, it's not like I'm hopeless without her."

"The thought never crossed my mind," said Toni.

Still, Olivia was the only person at camp who had a clue what my family was going through. So far I'd done fine on my own, but what if something changed? What if I fell apart?

I flashed back to Saturday afternoon, sitting on my bed, a slammed door shutting my parents out, my thumbs poised over my phone. I wondered how to put the news to Olivia. Her parents were so happy together. Under the shouts of every argument about who forgot to pick up a pound of pork, or whose turn it was to change the baby, flowed an unmistakable current of love. Could she ever understand what was happening to me?

Finally I typed, *My parents are splitting.* My fate boiled down to four words.

Olivia responded almost immediately. *WHAT?!?!?!?*

A moment later: *This makes no sense!!!*

Then: *I'M CALLING YOU.*

Sure enough, my phone began to ring, cruelly cheerful. "Melly! You weren't pranking me, were you? Your parents are breaking up?"

I gulped down my tears. "Yeah. I mean, no, it's the truth."

"But why?"

"They wouldn't say." It sounded so stupid. Stupid they hadn't told me, but also stupid I didn't know without being told. How clueless was I?

"You don't think one of them was having an affair, do you? Or maybe one of them has a gambling problem, or is an alcoholic."

"Olivia, you know my parents! They're the most boring people alive. Trust me, they don't have problems like that."

"I know, I know. But there's got to be a reason," she

insisted. "How can we fix this if we can't even figure out what's wrong?"

I knew she was right. There had to be a reason. But Mom and Dad were right, too. It didn't matter what the reason was because Olivia and I couldn't do anything about it. Nobody could, except for my parents, and it looked like they'd made up their minds not to. That Olivia thought she could waltz in and make things better was so typical.

"I'm coming over," she announced.

"I've got to pack," I said.

"So do I, but I kind of think this is more important!"

I imagined her flying over on her bike. Throwing her arms around me before launching into a rant about the injustice of grown-ups in general and my parents in particular. Maybe she wouldn't even make it to my room before confronting my parents, trying to persuade them to change their minds. She'd do it without stopping to breathe. I loved her for that.

But by then the raging pain I'd felt on hearing the news was dulling to a throbbing, bone-deep ache. I was exhausted. "Tomorrow," I told her. "I'll see you tomorrow."

"Okay," she said reluctantly, "but call me back if you need me."

"I will."

"Because I'm here for you. Always."

"I know," I'd said, meaning it.

And I did. Really. It was ridiculous to worry Olivia would forget all about me because of one little jam session with Noel.

Toni asked, "What are you going to do with yourself?"

"I'm not sure. I need to run through my band's songs, and I want to hit the percussion workshop. But I can't spend the entire afternoon playing or I'll go crazy."

"Come to the lake with me first. We can dive for rings."

"I can't dive," I said.

"Then jump," said Toni. "You've got to get in touch with nature, Melly. It'll put you in touch with your art."

I didn't know about that, but I was grateful for the invitation. I changed into my suit and slathered on sunscreen. Toni and I headed for the lake, flipping our picks on the way. A weight lifted from my shoulders as we walked the sun-dotted path to the beach. My steps felt light and springy. It occurred to me if I felt so good now, I must've felt pretty bad before without even knowing it.

As soon as we shed our shoes and towels, Toni took off running across the sand. When she reached the dock, she slowed to a brisk walk. "Come on!" she yelled over her shoulder. "What are you waiting for?"

My instincts told me to wade in slowly, like yesterday,

but I remembered Adeline saying it was easier if you ducked in all at once. So I followed Toni to the far end of the dock. She grabbed my hand. "Okay. On the count of three. One! Two!"

She yanked me over the edge. The shock of the cold water knocked the wind out of me. "You didn't get to three!" I sputtered.

Toni, treading water nearby, laughed her head off. "Your face! You should see it!"

"In touch with nature, my butt," I said. "You better sleep with one eye open tonight."

Toni cackled. "Ooo, I'm scared. I knew there was a tiger hiding inside that mouse of a girl."

The funny thing was, at that moment I sort of did feel like a tiger. I splashed water in Toni's face. Toni splashed me back, and then we were splash-fighting all the way out to the raft.

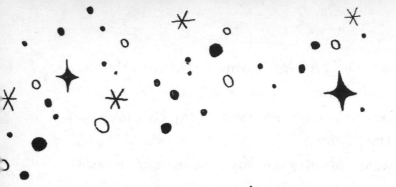

nine

Damon taught the percussion workshop himself. "Hey, I remember you," he said. "Good to see you here. How's the band situation?"

"It's okay," I said.

"I told you it would be, didn't I?" he said. "Would you—What's your name again?"

"Melly."

"Melly, since you're a little early, would you help me? I dragged out half the percussion instruments in the library, and any semblance of organization is shot."

Sure enough, there was a big pile sitting on the floor of the workshop cabin. This was only half of Camp Rockaway's percussion collection? How did they have space to store all this stuff? There were drums made of wood, drums made of clay. Drums with one head, drums with two. Gourds that rattled with seeds on the inside, and gourds wrapped with strings of beads on the outside. Instruments you could shake or pluck or strike together. I'd had no idea there were so many kinds.

About ten other kids, mostly boys, showed up for the workshop. Damon clapped his hands to get everyone's attention, and we sat in a circle. "Hey, rock stars," he said, "thanks for showing up to celebrate my favorite family of instruments. Not only that, the world's favorite family of instruments. Drums are found in virtually every culture on Earth, and you know why?"

"Because they're freaking awesome?" someone said. A chuckle rolled through the group.

Damon said, "That's right, man. Because they're freaking awesome. Whether they're part of a sacred ceremony or a halftime show, there's something elemental about them. Something intrinsic to the human experience. And you know why that is?"

No laughter this time. We shook our heads.

"Put a hand on your chest," Damon said. "Press it against your ribs. Feel what I feel?"

Under my palm, my heart beat strong and steady.

"You've got your very own drum inside you," Damon said, "and like calls to like. When you play, you're not just telling the drums what to do. They're talking back."

He let that sit with us a moment. A few kids rolled their eyes and nudged each other, and even I had to admit it sounded pretty cheesy. On the other hand, hadn't I felt just that way—that the drums weren't only an extension of my hands and feet, but also of my Self?

Damon broke the silence. "All right, enough of my New Age crap. Let's check out this crazy-cool stuff." He reached for the nearest drum and started telling us about it.

For the next hour, Damon introduced new instruments, demonstrated how to play them, and passed them around the circle so we could all try. They came from all over the world. The whole thing reminded me of Ms. Estrada's petting zoo, except the percussion instruments weren't hiding in the corner. They were center stage. They were everything.

I thought about what Damon said, that drums were the oldest instrument in the world, after the human voice. There's a stereotype that drummers are stupid and aggressive—like cavemen banging on rocks with their clubs. It's not true, obviously, not if you're any good. But what if cavemen *were* percussionists, in their own way? And what if it didn't mean they were stupid? What if they knew something amazing: what happens when you put your heart outside your body, where everyone can hear it?

When no one was looking, I pressed my hand to my ribs again, feeling part of something very big and very old and, yes, even sacred.

Damon caught my eye and winked. I ducked my head, but I was smiling.

Olivia wasn't in line outside the lodge when I arrived, but a bunch of other Treble Cliff girls were: Shauna and Toni, Adeline and Candace.

"Hey, Melly," Shauna said, waving me over. "Guess who's got two thumbs and just finished writing her first song of the summer?"

"Guess who hasn't shut up about it since?" Candace said. Shauna pouted, and Candace added, "I kid, I kid!"

"Is it about a country woman fighting the patriarchy?" I asked.

"Yes!" said Shauna. She started stomping her foot and sang in a drawling voice.

Hey mister, I don't like this plan yer pitchin'
You want me barefoot and pregnant, slavin' in the kitchen
I got my own job, and I got my own truck
You got a problem with that, then yer outta luck

"How old are you, again?" I asked.

"Thirteen. Why?"

"Well, the job. And the truck. And the pregnancy."

"I never said it was autobiographical," Shauna said. "Anyway, it's the principle of the thing. If women don't stand up for our rights, who will?"

She had a point.

"Hey, Melly," said Adeline, "I missed you at the lake today."

"Really?" I said, surprised she'd noticed, surprised she'd cared—but glad, too. My stomach did a little flip. "I went right after B-flat, with Toni."

"Darn. We must have just missed each other." She grinned. "One of these days."

"Absolutely!" I said. It came out louder than I meant. Everyone's eyes landed on me. *This. This is why you should never, ever open your mouth.*

To my relief, the line started moving. As we all grabbed a table together, Olivia ran up, skidding across the floor to squeeze into a chair between Shauna and me. "Hey," she said. "Miss me?" Her bangs were damp, and under her ponytail, sweat sparkled on her neck.

Would I sound like a bad friend if I said, *No, not really*? I'd been too busy to miss her, too busy to think about anything but what I was doing. Instead of answering, I said, "I'm glad you told me about the percussion workshop. I got to try a talking drum from West Africa. Its heads are connected by this leather cord. You hold it under your arm as you play, and depending on how tight you squeeze, it raises or lowers the pitch. It was so cool."

"It sounds like it," she said.

"What about you?" I asked, as bowls of turkey tetrazzini and green beans started making their way around the table. "Were you playing the entire time?"

Olivia plopped a heap of gooey noodles onto her plate. "Basically. We had to take a break in the middle because someone else signed out the room. So we just hung around outside until we could get back in."

"Nice," I said. I wasn't sure what else to say.

"Noel and I—we click, you know?" said Olivia. "It's just like you and me, except different. I don't know how to describe it. It's like there's this fizzy energy when we start playing. Like we're the only two people in the room."

"What about Brick?" I asked, nibbling a forkful of green beans.

"Oh, Brick. He's fine. And Noel invited this other guitar player, Mickey or Mikey or someone. He couldn't solo his way out of a paper bag. But it was okay because he was mainly playing rhythm. Noel's so much better."

"What kind of music did you play?" I asked. "More classic rock?"

Instantly Olivia's eyes were on her plate. She stirred her noodles. She mumbled something.

"What?" I said.

She raised her chin. "Don't laugh, Melly. Promise you won't laugh."

"Um. I promise?"

"The thing is, we played a lot of Grateful Dead."

"The Grateful Dead?" I repeated. "Didn't you once say they're a total grandpa band? Didn't you say their songs are the musical equivalent of stale bran muffins?"

The whole table went quiet. "Well," Shauna said, "tell us how you really feel."

"I'm sorry," I said in a low voice. "No offense to any Grateful Dead fans."

Everyone laughed—except Olivia. "All right, maybe I said those things," she said. "But nobody's perfect, right? And it doesn't really matter what we played. The point is we clicked."

"I know. I'm sorry," I said. "I'm glad you clicked."

"It's okay." She sighed. "Hopefully tomorrow we'll play something better."

I wondered if Noel had already asked her to jam again on Wednesday, or if Olivia was simply assuming. Either way, I didn't need to ask if she'd missed me. The answer was obvious. What I wasn't sure about was how that made me feel.

At the end of dinner, Damon took the stage to announce the next night's open mic and coffeehouse. "No actual coffee involved," Shauna said. Performing was a privilege reserved for junior high and high school campers, and even then there was a lottery. Everyone who wanted a chance to play could drop their name into an empty pickle jar, and Damon would draw the winners at breakfast.

"Remember, this event isn't just for solo acts," Damon said. "If you've got a group of friends you want to play with, it just takes one lucky winner to put you all on stage. There's one catch: to make sure as many people as possible get a chance to play, you can only perform once. And remember, if you don't get a turn this time, we're having another open mic next week."

Olivia grabbed my arm. "I am so going to put my name in. And if I get picked, I'll bring you on as my drummer. You should do it, too, Melly. We'll double our chances."

I remembered how I'd frozen at my audition, those measly five minutes with Donna in the practice cabin. Then I imagined myself freezing onstage in front of the entire camp. No thanks. Maybe by next week I'd feel ready, but I sure didn't now.

Besides, what if Olivia and I were both chosen? We wouldn't be able to play together. I'd have to ask David to be my bass player, and he'd probably tell me to forget it. If he even bothered answering.

Or what if Noel and I were chosen, and Noel wanted Olivia, too? What would happen if Olivia had to choose between us? Before today, I knew who she would've chosen. Now I wasn't sure. It was safer to keep my name out of the pickle jar.

"Maybe next week," I said.

Olivia joined the mob of campers writing their names on slips of paper with a Sharpie and tossing them into the pickle jar. Almost the entire table went up there, actually.

Adeline turned back. "You don't want to enter, Melly?"

I shook my head. "I don't think I'm ready."

"Are you kidding? You're great."

Now, that was a heap of baloney. I was barely keeping myself together during practice, much less the rest of the band. Adeline's tofu tetrazzini—tonight's vegetarian option—must have gone to her head. Still, I blushed. "Maybe next week," I repeated.

"Okay," Adeline said. "But if my name gets pulled, I'm asking you to be my drummer."

Suddenly I was presented with a new hypothetical: what if Olivia's and Adeline's names were both picked from the pickle jar?

ten

Olivia wasn't picked for the open mic. Neither was Adeline. Neither was anyone else who possibly would've asked me to play with them.

But Noel was one of the chosen few, and of course he asked Olivia to be his bass player. Her eyes sparkled as she turned to me. "Did you hear that, Melly? He wants me!"

"It would've been stranger if he'd asked someone else," I said. "It's not like he's been rubbing elbows with any other bass players."

"I know, I know. Still, there's something about hearing him say it, out loud, in front of all these people. It's like it's more real."

"Too bad he didn't call you up onstage first. Then everyone really would've heard him," I teased. "Anyway, I thought you were only in this for the music."

"Fine, mock me," Olivia said, sticking out her tongue. "I'll have you know, if someone you liked asked you to play, I'd be jumping up and down, shouting, 'Rah, rah, sis-boom-bah.'"

"In that case, thank goodness no one did," I said.

After running through our songs from Monday and Tuesday, Donna passed around our third chart. This time, I didn't recognize the name of the song. I didn't even recognize the name of the band. And when Donna pressed Play, I knew I'd never heard it before.

It started with tense, thumping drums. An electric guitar began to whine, softly as a mosquito, then growing in intensity, before breaking into chords as buzzy as a swarm of yellow jackets. The beat couldn't have been much simpler, like an exercise we might have played in fifth grade band. But the sound was anything but: distorted and dirty, jagged and rusty. It made yesterday's Metallica sound like polished chrome. And when the vocalist came in, her voice was a whiny holler.

"Rebel girl, rebel girl," she wailed, "rebel girl, you are the queen of my world."

Oh my God, Mom would HATE this! For some reason, the thought made me grin.

I double-checked the name of the band. Bikini Kill. Who were they, and why hadn't Olivia gotten any of their songs? Adeline was already mouthing the lyrics. Even Caleb was jerking his head along to the beat. This would teach him to dismiss music by women—though no one in their right mind would call this *chick music.* It wasn't the kind of girl power anthem you'd hear topping the charts, either. It was sassy and tough, just like the girl in the song, the rebel girl who ruled the neighborhood and didn't care if people called her names.

No wonder the singer adored her. So did I! She was everything I wasn't.

As the final chord twanged into dead air, Donna paused the stereo. She looked pleased. "Something tells me I picked a winner," she said. "What we've got here, people, is an American punk classic. If I had my way, I'd make it part of the national musical curriculum. But I'll settle for sharing it with you four. Let's sing it through with the recording, and then we'll dive in."

Right. Did I mention I don't dive? When it was time to pick up my sticks and play that noisy, don't-give-a-fig intro all on my own, every muscle in my back and shoulders knotted. I did my best to block out the rest of the band, especially Donna, letting everything blur but the black and white of my chart. I brought down my sticks, and sound burst from my drums, but I could tell right away it was all wrong.

The drummer on the recording swaggered in torn-up

jeans. She stomped in steel-toed boots. Me? I was practically tiptoeing, my back pressed against the wall.

Donna knew it, too. The rest of the group had barely joined in when she called, "This isn't school, Melly! This is rock and roll. Pump up the volume. Loosen up."

I knew she was trying to help, in her way. But it was exactly the wrong thing to say. My shoulders tensed even more. How could I loosen up when she was focusing all her attention on me? Maybe I was a little stiff, but at least I was playing in time, which was more than I could say for David, who was off in his own little world, or Caleb, who was half a measure ahead. Didn't Donna get it? I was already playing as hard as I could! She could have me quiet and in control, or she could have me loud and . . . well, I didn't know, because I didn't *do* loud. Because even thinking about it made my heart beat too fast and my stomach somersault, and I heard a roar like my ears were pressed to an enormous seashell.

Maybe she realized she'd made a mistake. Over the rest of practice, she gave the others notes and told us, "Sing, people. No, scratch that, scream!" But she didn't single me out again. She didn't even make eye contact with me, though that might have been my fault. I kept my eyes down. I didn't want to see her disappointment that I was the opposite of a rebel girl. I didn't want to hear her thinking that I should be playing the piccolo instead of the drums.

Poppy handed me a letter during B-flat. I stared at it. I'd been waiting for three days, and now it was here. The address was printed in purple gel pen, in Mom's handwriting. I didn't want to read it. Well, I did and I didn't. I wanted to know what it said, but I was afraid. It could say anything, anything at all.

"Just open it," Olivia whispered.

I shoved my thumb under the flap and ripped it open. The stationery had a border of little black-and-white cats that looked a lot like Maki. Mom wasn't much of a letter writer. She must have bought the paper specially to write to me at camp.

Dear Melly,

It's Sunday night, and I've just made myself some chamomile tea and queued up Gilmore Girls. Only two hours on Route 131, but it feels like you're on the other side of the world. Maki's been sniffing around your room, wondering where you are.

In some ways, tomorrow will be back to normal: work, etc. Except your father has signed the lease to a new apartment. He's spending tomorrow night there. So it will be extra quiet.

I hope you, on the other hand, are making lots of noise and having fun! Did you find the stationery? I would love to hear about your band. Do you have time for anything besides music, music, music?

Lots of love,

Mom

My heart squeezed in on itself. The letter felt like a message in a bottle, tossed into the sea a hundred years ago. When Mom was writing that letter, I was at the concert the first night of camp. While Dad was settling into bed at his new apartment with a book or his laptop, I was hiking back to my tent after firebowl. What else had happened, what else had changed, that I wouldn't hear about for days to come?

The worst thing was realizing that by the time I got back home, Dad would be completely moved out. I imagined the house with all the pieces of him removed. In my mind, it looked like Swiss cheese, but with more holes than cheese. What were we going to eat when he was gone, anyway? Mom was probably stuffing the freezer with Stouffer's lasagna. The fanciest meal she'd ever made involved canned tuna and mayonnaise.

Or maybe the worst thing was wondering why Dad hadn't written to me, too.

"Everything okay?" Olivia asked softly.

I blinked back the tears that sparked in my eyes.

"Yeah, I guess." I shoved the letter back into its envelope, crumpled the whole thing into a ball, and leaned over the side of my bed, shoving it into the bottom of my suitcase.

"You want to talk about it?" Olivia said.

Part of me did. With each band practice and campfire and trip to the lake, I was piling sandbags to keep my jostling emotions at bay. But at times like this I could feel them rising. How long before one big surge sent them over the wall? Just the same, I shook my head. What could I tell Olivia besides, *Life doesn't make sense anymore, and I hate it*?

She waited a moment longer, then rolled over onto her back. "So, what do you think I should wear for the open mic? I was thinking my black jeans and my Camp Rockaway shirt, the one I ordered when I signed up for camp. But probably it's hokey to wear a camp shirt at a camp show. And it's red. What if it clashes with my bass? What about my turquoise tank top? Basic, but in a good way . . . right?"

My stomach ached like I'd been punched. I wasn't sure what hurt more, Mom's letter or Olivia's cluelessness.

I decided to go to the meadow. I could go to a far corner and bury my nose in *The Beat of My Own Drum,* and no one could see I was actually crying. When B-flat ended,

I grabbed my book and water bottle and headed to the Fretboard to flip my pick.

Stepping along the path from the woods into the meadow was like stepping from spring into summer. The sun blazed down. The air went from cool and piny to warm and grassy sweet. I walked along the edge, where the mown part of the field met tall brush and bright spatters of wildflowers. I passed a kid shooting hoops by himself on the paved half-court, and others starting up a game of touch football.

I found my quiet corner at the far end of the field. The shouts and laughs of the other campers faded. Insect song swallowed me whole. Cicadas and something else, maybe grasshoppers? And the whine of a mosquito! I was glad I'd remembered to put on more bug spray before leaving my tent. I settled cross-legged in the stiff, dry grass and opened my book.

But each time my eyes focused on the letters, they floated off the page, hovering and shimmering like a cloud of gnats. My heart hurt so much. How could I make it through another ten days at camp as Dad emptied out our house of his things, of himself? How could I make it through the rest of my life with my family broken into pieces? The gnats dissolved altogether as my eyes went blurry.

I didn't hear the footsteps crunching across the meadow almost until two sneakers stopped in front of me, two white socks giving way to brown ankles. Adeline.

She set down her guitar case and knelt. "Hey. You okay?"

I closed Sheila E. "I was just reading." My voice wavered. Stupid voice.

"Do you want to talk about what's wrong?"

People's parents got divorced every day. If I started telling Adeline about it, I'd probably start crying again, and she'd think I was totally juvenile. Besides, my best friend had just offered to talk, and hadn't I told her no? Why would I turn around and share my sad story with someone I barely knew? I shook my head.

"Is it about camp? You seemed kind of down during practice this morning."

I shook my head again.

"Okay. Because if it was, I'd be happy to knock some heads together for you. Especially if it was Caleb. In fact, maybe I'll knock his head against something just for kicks."

I smiled and sniffed. It turned into sort of a wet, noisy snort. When Adeline grinned instead of getting grossed out, I decided maybe I could trust her after all. "My parents are getting divorced."

"Oh." Adeline sank all the way to the ground. "That sucks."

"They told me right before camp."

"Seriously? Right before camp? Like, 'We're getting divorced, see you in two weeks'?"

"Basically. It was the day before. But still." I took a deep breath. "I'm going to go home, and my dad's going to be gone." I couldn't help it. I started crying again—quietly, but there were definitely tears spilling from my eyes. Those sandbags were goners.

Adeline waited a minute in silence. Then she said, "I'm sorry, Melly."

Somehow, it was exactly what I needed to hear. It didn't magically fix everything, and yet, by acknowledging that things *weren't* okay, it made me feel a little bit better.

"I wish I had a tissue to give you," she said. "That's the least I could do, right?"

"I'd use a leaf, but I'd probably pick poison ivy." I brushed my sleeve across my eyes.

"Ah, now that I could help you with. My granny's granny taught her all about plants, and now she's teaching me. The good, the bad, and the itchy."

"Oh, yeah?" My voice still quavered but was mostly back under control. "What's that little plant there, with the round leaves and the bumpy little stalks coming out the top?" I pointed. "I see it all the time back home, but my parents say it's just a weed."

"Just a weed!" Adeline said, throwing up her hands

in mock horror. "I'll have you know that weed—which is called plantain, by the way—is good for all kinds of things. Sores. Bee stings. Diar-freaking-rhea. Can anything at Walgreens treat all that?"

I shook my head.

"And see those little trees with the cones of red berries? That's sumac. You can make juice out of the berries. They're full of antioxidants—and, okay, I'm not entirely clear on what those are, but I know they're good for you. When I was a kid, I'd try to eat them, but they're really sour. And fuzzy."

"And poison ivy?" I said.

"Oh, you definitely shouldn't eat that."

We both laughed.

"Honestly, camp is crawling with it," Adeline said. "Have you ever heard, 'Leaves of three, let it be'? There are plenty of harmless plants with clusters of three leaves. But you don't want to learn the difference the hard way. If I see any, I'll point it out to you, so you're prepared the next time you need to blow your nose."

I rolled my eyes. "Thanks."

"Do you really want to read that book? Because I can leave you alone. But if you wanted, maybe we could do something else."

"What about you? You must have come here for a reason." I nodded at her guitar.

"It can wait. Besides, it takes two to canoe."

"Canoe?"

"When I need to clear my mind of all the junk, I like to take a boat and go out on the lake. Nowhere else beats it for real peace and quiet."

"Here's pretty good, too," I said.

"Until random weirdos come up and start bothering you, right?" Adeline extended her shoe and tapped it against mine. It sent a tickle up my leg. "Obviously you don't have to, but if you'd be up for it . . . I'd like that. And I think you'd like it, too."

I raised my eyebrows. "What makes you think that?"

"Oh, I don't know. I guess there's something about you."

Adeline was only teasing again. I knew that. But something about her tone, and the way her brown eyes sparkled, sent a flutter through my stomach—like how the wind rustles through a pile of leaves, sending them dancing into the air for a moment before they drift back to the ground. I looked at her hard, trying to understand. But I wasn't sure what I was looking for, so how was I supposed to recognize it when I saw it?

Whatever. She was right: I was done stewing. I was ready for peace. "Okay. I'm in."

Adeline hopped up and held out a hand. Leaves swirling inside me, I took it.

eleven

At **Joan Jetty**, Adeline waved at the bronze-skinned, ponytailed counsclor standing ankle deep in the water, peering out at the few boats already on the lake: a rowboat, a couple of canoes, a kayak. "Hey, Skip. Melly and I are going to take out a canoe, okay?"

"Great," Skip said. She waded back onto the shore. "Have you ever paddled a canoe before, Melly?"

"Um, no."

"Don't worry. You'll be in good hands with Adeline. Can I see your arm?"

Confused, I held out an arm. Skip took it by the wrist and turned it this way and that. "Yep, put this girl in the front of the canoe. She'll be a powerhouse."

"What do you mean?" I asked.

"She means you're strong," Adeline said. "Melly's a drummer."

"That explains it," Skip said. "In a nutshell, Melly: person in the front of the canoe's the motor. Good to have lots of power up there. Person in the back's the steering wheel. In any case, it's good for the more experienced paddler to sit in back. Less chance you'll end up in a patch of stinging nettles."

"Don't scare her. Besides, I've told you, nettles are more helpful than harmful." Adeline winked at me. I wasn't sure how long she'd been coming to Camp Rockaway, but it was obvious she'd known Skip quite a while. I didn't think I could ever talk to a grown-up the way Adeline was talking to Skip—almost like they were friends. But then, Adeline often sounded older than most thirteen-year-olds I knew. I wondered why. Was she just naturally mature or something?

"Helpful or not," Skip said, "you don't want the rash that comes with them. If you're going to get stuck somewhere, let it be in a patch of water lilies. Just don't—"

"Pick them. We know, we know," Adeline said. "Take only pictures. Leave only footprints. I'm sure you were a wonderful Girl Scout, Skip."

"Thanks, smart mouth. Since you mention it, I was."

We took off our shoes and socks. Skip helped us find life jackets and paddles in the boathouse. There was already a line of canoes sitting at the water's edge, half in and half out of the water. Skip demonstrated how to paddle and get in and out, crouching so the canoe wouldn't tip too much.

"All right, all right," Adeline said. "Before the sun sets."

Skip turned to me. "Does she talk to everyone this way, or am I special?" I shrugged, and she laughed. "Rhetorical question, Melly. Climb in. I'll push you off."

Adeline climbed in first, moving to the back. I sat in front, balancing the paddle across my knees. Skip lifted the bow out of the sand and pushed us into the water. "Have fun out there," she said, "and remember, three long whistles means it's time to come back to shore."

I paddled backward: dip, push, lift. Even though the motion felt awkward, the canoe sliced through the water surprisingly fast. When we cleared the swimming area, Adeline called, "We should be able to turn around now."

"What do I do?"

"Nothing! Just start paddling forward. I'm steering, remember?"

Sure enough, the canoe's nose swung gently to the left. I found my rhythm, dipping the paddle alongside the canoe and pulling backward in a strong, smooth motion. Then I lifted and swung the paddle around to the front. Water dripped from its blade in a little semicircle. It was hard work, but it was also relaxing. As we

moved away from the bustle at shore, I began to understand why Adeline liked it.

We paddled toward an area where the trees looked
especially thick. "Where we're pointed?" Adeline said.
"That's the border between Camp Rockaway and the
sheep farm."

"Do we have to stay on this side?" I asked.

"Nope. The whole lake is fair game. But if we were
to land on that side—well, I've heard some of those
sheep farmers can be pretty grumpy."

"Yeah?"

"Yep. I heard if they catch you on their property
they'll take a pair of shears and give you the haircut of
your life." I looked over my shoulder. As usual, Adeline
was grinning.

I smiled back but confessed, "My shoulder's getting
tired."

"Switch sides," she said. "Or if both sides are tired,
rest. We've got nowhere to be."

"I can keep going for a while," I said, switching my
paddle to the other side of the canoe. But I paddled
slower. Adeline was right. There was no reason to hurry.

She steered us along the shore, close enough to get
a good look at the cattails and water lilies that grew
there but not close enough to get tangled up. Though
the air was muggy, I didn't notice any mosquitoes. I saw

little flies with emerald armor and insects with long, blue slivers of bodies and long black wings—like dragonflies, but more delicate. I pointed one out to Adeline.

"They're called damselflies," she said. "They come out here to hunt."

"Hunt?" I hunched my shoulders like I could protect myself.

"Other insects, not people. Beautiful but deadly," she said cheerfully.

"How do you know all this nature stuff?" I asked. "Is it because of your grandma?"

"Partly. But also I grew up in the middle of nowhere, which helps. I'm from the UP, outside Marquette."

Marquette. I remembered the name from her T-shirt the other day. I'd never been to the Upper Peninsula, but I nodded as if I knew just where she meant.

"What about you?" Adeline asked. "City girl, I'm guessing. Grand Rapids? Detroit?"

"Kalamazoo." I rested my paddle on my knees and held up a hand to make the Lower Peninsula's mitten shape, pointing to where Kalamazoo would be. "It's not even a big city, but my parents are not remotely outdoorsy. Canoeing would blow their minds."

Immediately I shoved the thought of them away. I was out on the lake specifically not to think about them. Silently we rocked, drifting with the breeze.

"How'd you end up at camp?" Adeline asked. "I'm guessing it wasn't your parents' idea."

"It was Olivia's."

"And she dragged you along, too?"

"She didn't drag me," I said quickly. "I wanted to come. We're best friends."

"Relax," Adeline said. "I was kidding. Hey." A little splash of water hit my elbow, and I turned to see water dribbling from her fingers. "I'm really glad you're here. You're cool."

"Nobody in my life has ever accused me of being cool," I said.

"What? That doesn't seem possible. I've been coming to Camp Rockaway since I was eight. I'm the expert on cool."

"Wow," I said. "That long?"

"Yep. This is my vacation every year."

"From school?"

"From the rest of my life."

I looked at her blankly. Adeline seemed way too chipper to have a troubled life. Then again, if you judged by *Anne of Green Gables, Heidi,* and *Pollyanna,* the world's chipperest people were orphans, so go figure.

"My dad's got PPMS. Primary progressive multiple sclerosis," she said, as if that explained it. I knew multiple sclerosis was a kind of disease, but I didn't know what the rest of it meant. I guessed it was especially bad. "I have to help out a lot at home, especially in the summer. Babysitting for my little brothers, cleaning house, that kind of thing."

"Oh." There was my answer about why Adeline sounded more grown-up than I did. She was. "Is your dad—is that why you came to camp in a taxi?"

"Getting around can be hard for him sometimes, and so can the heat. He's got a wheelchair if he's tired and sore, but the trails here aren't the best for that. Add in a long drive with three kids. . . . It's a lot to deal with." Adeline shrugged. "So they stick me on a bus to Cadillac, and I take a taxi the rest of the way. It works."

"Will you have to take a bus home, too?" I asked. It seemed like such a lonely journey, all the way from the UP and back, no one from her family to cheer her on at the final show.

"Nah, it's all good. Everyone'll be here for the show—even my granny! My point is, I can't do a thing about dirty dishes or skinned knees while I'm here. It's my parents' gift to me, and I try to enjoy every minute of it, you know? Anyway, we better start moving or we'll be in danger of hitting those nettles Skip warned us about."

I picked up my paddle, and Adeline turned the canoe so we faced into the sun. She started humming a tune I didn't recognize. "What is that?" I asked.

"Just a song," Adeline said. "Am I bothering you?"

"Nope," I said, "it's pretty."

I squinted ahead, then closed my eyes. I felt like we'd floated into an alternate universe, one without any drama—not my parents', not Olivia's, not even my own. I didn't need to steer right now. All I had to do was paddle.

twelve

Everyone dressed up for the open mic—as much as we could in the middle of the woods. I settled for a fresh pair of jeans and a clean T-shirt, but my bunkmates spent the better part of an hour getting ready: choosing outfits, doing hair, putting on makeup. Toni had a whole kit stashed in her suitcase, and she was happy to play the role of tent cosmetologist.

Olivia's eyes were bright, almost feverish. "Oh my God. I am so nervous," she said, pulling a brush through her hair for what seemed like the thousandth time. It was going to come out by the roots soon. "I wish there was somewhere to plug in a curling iron."

"Did you bring yours?" I asked.

"No, because I knew there was nowhere to plug one in. But I've got to do something about my hair. I wish you were better at hair, Melly!"

"Sorry," I said. "Maybe Toni or Shauna can help you out."

"I've got you covered," Shauna said, producing a bag full of bobby pins, clips, and elastics. "With hair like mine, you've got to be prepared."

She swept Olivia's hair into an updo with a bunch of hair spiking out of the top. It looked like a firecracker. Olivia loved it.

"Come on, Mel," said Shauna, "can't I do yours, too?"

"It's too short to do anything with," I said. "Trust me, I've tried."

"At least let me put in a couple of butterfly clips," Shauna said.

"And you need glitter," Toni said. "Friends don't let friends go out without a little sparkle."

When Blair hollered for us to meet up in the fire circle, we all looked ready for a party, our skin glinting in the sinking pink sun.

The lights in the lodge were dim. Even the stage lights were low. Instead, an odd assortment of lamps surrounded the stage, and white holiday lights adorned the mic stands. Votive candles flickered at the tables. Everything had a cozy glow. Soft music played over the sound system.

Someone tall waved at us from across the hall, in front of the stage. "There's Noel and the guys!" Olivia said. "Come on, Melly."

I hurried after her. But by the time we reached them, there was only one chair left at Noel's table.

"Hey, Olivia," he said. His eyes skimmed over me to settle on her. I looked down at myself to make sure I was really there. Yep—just not important enough to warrant a greeting, apparently. "I'm sorry, I only saved enough seats for the band. Maybe you and your friend can sit at the next table."

Olivia hesitated only a moment. "No," she said, "that's okay. Melly understands, right, Mel? It's more important for me to sit with the band. Band solidarity. You get it, right, Melly?"

"It's fine," I said. *At least he should know my name now.* "I'll find Toni and Shauna."

"Thanks for understanding," Olivia said, giving me a quick hug. "Wish me luck?"

"Luck," I said with a quiet sigh, and she slid into the chair beside Noel.

I looked around the lodge, feeling lost. Toni and Shauna's table was already full. I stood helplessly in the middle of the hall, looking for an empty chair next to someone I knew. I was about to give up and sit with a bunch of eight-year-old boys, steeling myself for two hours of fart jokes, when Adeline popped up a couple of tables away. "Melly! Over here." She made someone scoot over so I could have the seat beside her.

"You didn't have to do that," I told the girl who'd moved.

"Oh, Yasmina doesn't mind, do you, Mina?" Adeline said.

It was an uncomfortable echo of Olivia's words to Noel. But the other girl shook her head with a grin. She had long, curly black hair streaked with neon pink. I'd seen her around, but she wasn't in Treble Cliff.

"Hi," she said. "Yasmina. Any friend of Adeline's—well, you fill in the rest."

Just then Poppy stopped by our table with a pad of paper in her hand and a pen tucked over her ear. "Welcome to Café Rockaway," she said. "May I take your drink order? We've got hot chocolate, lemonade, and water."

Yasmina ordered lemonade. Adeline and I ordered hot chocolate. It wasn't cold out, not at all. But hot chocolate was comforting, and I was in the mood to be comforted. It didn't really bother me that Olivia wanted to sit with her band. That made total sense. But I hated the way she'd completely forgotten me the moment Noel entered her field of vision. I hated pretending the whole thing was about music and not her crush on Noel.

Adeline's voice dragged my thoughts back to our table. "Mina and I were in the same band last year, which was awesome. But then she had to go and have another birthday, so she got bumped up to Carole King-dom and left me behind."

"Sorry!" Yasmina said. "But you're obviously doing okay without me." She turned to me. "Adoline's told me great things about you."

"She's exaggerating," I said. I hadn't meant it to be funny, but both Yasmina and Adeline giggled. "It's true!" I protested, and they giggled even harder.

"How can you know she's exaggerating? You don't even know what she said," Yasmina pointed out. "Maybe she was praising your excellent hygiene."

"Out here in the woods, the bar is set pretty low," Adeline joked.

"Or maybe she's impressed by your teeth, which you have to admit are exceptionally straight. You should've seen Addy's before those braces. They looked like—"

"Enough!" Adeline slapped the table. "My orthodontia is not up for discussion. But it's true, Melly, your teeth are very nice. Good job."

"Okay, okay." I laughed. "Point taken."

"The real issue is that Melly sells herself short," Adeline told Yasmina. "She's already figured out what some people never do: how to play in a band."

"What are you talking about?" I said. "I'm no better than Caleb or David—especially Caleb. He's been playing forever."

"I'm not talking about how to play the songs,"

Adeline said. "I'm talking about how to play with other people. There's a huge difference."

Yasmina said, "Anyone can pick up an instrument, Melly. Not everyone knows how to listen. Music's a conversation. It doesn't work if everyone's just talking to themselves."

They were both watching me, as if they expected me to shout, *Eureka! It's clear to me now.* But it wasn't. My entire life, listening was never my problem. My problem was figuring out what to say and getting up the nerve to say it.

I shook my head. "You two sound like Damon and Donna's love children," I said, and this time I did mean to be funny, because otherwise they'd know how stupid I felt.

Sure enough, Adeline burst out laughing. "And you're funny," she said. "Yasmina, didn't I tell you she was funny?" She reached out and squeezed my wrist.

Something strange happened. A current passed from her fingers into me. It buzzed all the way up my arm to my shoulder, then all the way down to my toes. As it went, it grew—as if a single honeybee had flown in and multiplied into a swarm. My heart was a hive. It hummed.

Then Adeline's fingers were back in her own lap, but still I felt their pressure on my arm. I looked down to see if they'd left a mark. But I only saw shadows flickering on my skin in the candlelight.

As Damon announced the first act, I settled back in my chair and prepared to soak up the sound. And mostly I succeeded: relaxing into the groove when things were going well, wincing when they weren't. But my mind was never completely on the music, even when Olivia took the stage with Noel and his friends to play their ode to Jerry Garcia and I sat up straight to pay attention.

Because I couldn't not see Adeline out of the corner of my eye. Couldn't not feel the warmth of her a few inches away. Couldn't not wonder why my heart would not slow down.

Olivia leaped on me on our hike back to Treble Cliff, linking elbows with me. "What did you think?"

"You were sensational," I said.

"Brick flubbed the lead-in," she said. "You never would've done that!"

"Maybe I would've."

"Okay. Maybe. But you wouldn't have turned around and blamed it on me."

"That's true. Anyway, I don't think anyone noticed."

"Oh, they noticed," Olivia said. "How could they not?"

"Nobody cares," I said. "It's not a contest, remember? And you just started playing together a couple of days ago."

Olivia sighed and dipped her head against my shoulder. "All right. You're trying to make me feel better, and I should let you, huh?"

"Yes, you should."

"Okay. I will accept your word that we did not completely suck."

"Definitely not. Just think, if you sounded this good on Day Four, you'll be amazing by the show on Day Fourteen."

"Thanks, Mel," Olivia said. "You always make me feel better."

I was glad, but also exhausted. How could such small problems require so much energy? And maybe it was selfish to think it, but what had happened to her making *me* feel better?

That's not fair. She asked if you wanted to talk today. You're the one who said no.

Which was confusing. Why had my feelings been too snarled up to share with Olivia? Why had they flowed out when Adeline found me in the meadow? It didn't make sense. Had I forgotten who my best friend was?

Olivia started picking through each performance, from choice of songs to choice of outfits to actual execution. I tried to listen, but my mind wandered away. My feet felt funny and numb, like they couldn't quite make contact with the ground. My head was floating somewhere high above, bobbing along like a balloon.

My body continued to walk to the campsite, but my soul drifted back down the path to the lodge, back to my seat between Adeline and Yasmina. I felt the happiness and confusion that Adeline had thought me worth telling Yasmina about. I felt the warm pressure of her fingers. My soul vibrated like a snare.

"Earth to Melly," Olivia said, and my soul careened back up the path and snapped back into my chest. "What did you do today? I was so obsessed with the open mic, I forgot to ask."

"Just hung out," I said. My ears were ringing, as if they'd been stuffed with cotton and Olivia had yanked it out. The cacophony of frogs and toads and crickets and campers' voices deafened me. I wasn't quite sure why I didn't mention canoeing with Adeline, but something inside me resisted. "A little of this. A little of that."

Olivia nodded. "Well, if you're ever feeling lonely, you should come grab me."

"I will," I said. I wondered if she meant it. I wondered if I'd want to try.

thirteen

My pulse sped up when I saw Adeline at band practice, but she only gave me her usual smile. "Ready for another grueling session?" she asked.

If she was acting like everything was normal, I'd try to act normal, too. I rolled my eyes. "Does it matter, either way?" I slid behind the drums to make my daily height adjustments to everything. Whoever played right before me must've been a hobbit.

She giggled. "Fair point. Donna does seem to enjoy keeping us on our toes."

That was one way of putting it. From pop to heavy metal to riot grrrl punk, Donna had picked songs that went together like peanut butter and Cheez Whiz. And today the pattern—or lack of it—continued.

I recognized the new song as soon as Donna put it on the stereo, probably from Mom's favorite station for the car, the one that played "all your favorite hits of yesterday, today, and tomorrow!" It was called "Landslide," and it started with a single acoustic guitar—no strumming, just the same pattern picked lightly over each chord—and a woman's wistful voice. The song built gradually, a second acoustic harmonizing with the first, then a haunting solo on electric that reminded me of the wind moaning at the eaves of our house on a stormy night.

If you'd asked me to explain every line, I couldn't have told you. The woman sang about snow-covered hills one minute, and the ocean the next. But somehow the meaning was clear to me. It was about change, and how confusing and risky and scary it was, because you never knew when that next step would send an avalanche tumbling down and burying you alive.

Hunched on my stool, I felt paralyzed, but also like I wanted to jump up and yell, *Yes! This is totally my life!* Coming to camp 150 miles from home. My parents divorcing. Things being weird with Olivia. Things being a different kind of weird with Adeline. If anyone was caught in a landslide, it was me. Donna said she'd picked a song with each of us in mind, and I didn't know how she could've guessed what was happening to me, but I *knew* it was mine.

I guess it didn't speak to everyone, though, because

as soon as it was over, Caleb demanded, "What are we supposed to do with that?"

"Whatever do you mean?" Donna asked, the way she did when she knew exactly what you meant but wasn't going to give you the satisfaction of admitting it.

"There's only, like, ten seconds of electric guitar, for starters," he said. "There's no bass. There's no drums. It's all acoustic and vocals—solo vocals."

"Oh," Donna said. "Thanks for pointing that out. That's very observant of you."

Caleb crossed his arms over his chest, his lips pinched. I felt a little sorry for him. I hated when teachers were sarcastic. If Donna had spoken to me that way, I'd be mortified. Forget those 150 miles. I'd grab my sticks and start walking home. Besides, he had a point.

On the other hand, after yesterday I was mostly relieved Donna wasn't picking on me.

To my surprise, Adeline came to Caleb's defense. "I've heard dozens of covers of 'Landslide,' and it's always acoustic and vocals. If it's really out there, banjo or violin."

"Anyone else?" Donna asked. Her eyes homed in on me. "Melly? What do you think: can 'Landslide' be performed with a full band?"

"Maybe it could, technically." I hesitated. "But it wouldn't respect the songwriter's intentions, right?"

Donna turned to David. He, naturally, shrugged.

"Wow," Donna said, "okay. Let's talk about this. Remember listening to 'Enter Sandman' the other day?" Everyone nodded. "Great. So I assume you remember that awesome rhythm part on acoustic."

We looked at each other. "Uh, there wasn't one," Adeline said.

"Oh, really? That's interesting. My mistake. What about Monday, when David played that really beautiful keyboard line, just like on the recording?"

Nobody bothered saying David didn't have a keyboard. We knew Donna was messing with us. We just hadn't figured out why.

Donna sighed. "People. You are but one little four-piece band in the middle of the woods. You could be geniuses, and you would never be able to replicate everything you hear on these recordings. You've been improvising all week to make up for differences in instrumentation and musical proficiency. Today is no different."

"But 'Landslide' is basically perfect as is," Adeline said. I nodded.

"What's the problem?" Donna said. "You're afraid of offending Stevie Nicks, who wrote that song probably before your parents were born? Trust me, I think she can handle it."

"But there's barely anything to work with!" Caleb protested. "Where do we even start?"

"You say there's less to work with," Donna said. "I say there's more opportunities for you to be creative. Look. Playing with new people gives you the chance to experiment with a new sound. This is your chance to blaze a trail. To be different from everyone who's come before you. Don't waste it. Start hashing it out."

When she put it that way, it sounded exciting, but also scary. Since when had I been a trailblazer? Oh wait—since never!

"I think we should keep the fingerpicking," Adeline said. "It's essential. But what are we going to do with the rest of you?"

"I want more than that solo," Caleb said. "I didn't come to camp to stand here with my teeth in my mouth."

"Sure," said Adeline. "Why don't you work out a new guitar part? You could come in on the second verse, like on the recording, but doing your own thing."

Telling Caleb to do his own thing sounded like a dangerous proposition, but Adeline was obviously trying to keep things positive. "What about David and me?" I said. "Should we come in on the second verse, too?"

"Sure," Adeline said. "Maybe you could start quiet, but get louder as the song goes on."

"I've actually got just the tools for that," I said. I

rummaged in my stick bag for my brushes, popping the long wire bristles out through their plastic handles.

Caleb squinted. "What are those?"

"Brushes. I've barely ever used them. My mom got them because she heard they were quieter than sticks—which they are—but they're also not, like, hard rock material." I smiled. "But I think they'll do the job here. I can switch back to sticks if we want to kick it up a notch."

"Great idea!" Adeline said, and I went pink with pride. "That leaves David."

"Come in at the same time as me," I told him, feeling more sure of myself with Adeline as my ally. "The rhythm section needs to stick together."

"And we've got the chords," Adeline said. "Maybe you could do something super simple, like this—" She sang what she was thinking, just one note per measure: *dum, dum, dum, dum.*

David seemed relieved by how easy it was. "I could do something like that," he agreed.

It wasn't magic from that point on. Adeline was still the only one who could sing and play at the same time with any real confidence. But she stopped trying to blend so much and started singing out, and it helped. The louder she sang, the more the lyrics sank into my brain, until the words materialized in my mouth and I could put more of my energy into the drums. It helped that the song called for a light touch. I could do light.

It had its challenges, though, mostly because David wouldn't make eye contact with me. Yasmina said playing in a band was like having a conversation? Well, you can't have a conversation if the other person refuses to talk to you, or even look at you. I was tired of struggling to interpret his head bobs and chin thrusts. Instead, I laid down the beat as if I were playing alone. David would catch up, or not.

Occasionally Donna chimed in with suggestions, including multiple requests for Caleb to chill out and let the lyrics do the heavy lifting, but if she noticed any problems with David and me, she didn't mention them. For the most part she stayed out of the way. When her watch beeped, she said, "Yes, people, yes. You are starting to sound like a band."

I actually sort of agreed.

I got another surprise when Adeline asked, "You want to hang out this afternoon?"

"Oh! Yeah! I think? Maybe?" I slid my brushes into my stick bag and zipped it up.

"Sorry. I forgot you probably need to check with Olivia."

Adeline didn't say it in a mean way, but her words were a wake-up call. *Did* I need to check with Olivia?

It was pretty clear she had her own agenda, one that didn't include me. Why should I wait to see what she was doing before I made my own plans?

"No, actually, I don't," I said. "Scratch the maybe. I'd love to hang out."

Adeline smiled, but it wasn't the big, beaming smile I'd come to expect. It was quieter—sort of bashful. If she were someone else, I'd almost think it was shy. "I've got some stuff I need to do right after B-flat," she said. "But do you want to go to the beach after that? Or if you had something else in mind, and didn't mind some company . . ."

"Beach sounds good," I said before I could start feeling shy myself. "What time?"

No surprise, Olivia had made plans to play with Noel. With both her and Adeline busy, I had the first half of the afternoon all to myself. First I ran through our band's songs. Then I went to the crafts cabin, where I stayed long enough to make a key chain. It was kid stuff: pressing acorns and twigs and things into clay, then poking a hole for the key ring. I used a pair of maple seeds on one side and scratched my initials on the other. It would make a good ID tag for my stick bag. The crafts counselor told me I could pick it up the next day, after it had been baked.

"Want to make another?" she asked. "Something for your best friend back home?"

"My best friend is here at camp."

"That's lucky. A brother or sister?"

"I don't have any."

"Well, what about your parents?"

Ha. "I don't think so," I said. There hadn't been any letters for me at B-flat. The running total was still one from Mom, zero from Dad.

It was time to go to the lake. I flipped my pick on the way to Treble Cliff to put on my swimsuit. Adeline's pick hung in the workshop column. I looked for Olivia's next. It was hanging in the lodge column, of course. It never seemed to budge.

Toni was changing into her own suit when I arrived at our tent. "Melly. What's up?"

"I'm going swimming. Are you going, too?"

"Nah," Toni said, "I heard they're having Miss America tryouts at the lodge." She flung out one arm, pointing a toe and thrusting out her chest. We both burst out laughing.

We walked to the beach together. This time, Toni jumped right off the end of the dock and headed for the raft without waiting to see if I'd follow. I went at my own pace, soaking up the sun. I dipped a toe into the water by the shore. It was perfect. I wandered to the end of the dock and, instead of jumping, lowered myself slowly down the ladder, the water creeping up my legs and then my middle, until it engulfed me. Only then did I paddle out to the raft.

The perfect moment shattered. The raft was crowded with loud, dripping kids. Shauna was one of them. She yelled, "Melly! We're having a contest. Doofus here is under the impression boys dive better than girls, and I think we all know that's a steaming pile of—"

"I can't dive," I mumbled, ashamed.

"So be a judge," she said. "We've got more girls than boys, anyway."

"She can't judge," the doofus said. "She'll be biased toward the girls."

"Don't be ridiculous," said Shauna. "Melly will be objective."

"We should have two judges," he insisted. "A boy and a girl."

"Then going by your logic—which isn't, by the way, remotely logical—it'll always come out a tie."

"Then we need a tiebreaker judge."

"Argh!" Shauna said. "Who do you suggest?"

"A sheep!" Toni yelled. The crowd groaned and laughed.

I was regretting having come to the beach. I wasn't sure what I wanted, but it wasn't this chaos. Where was Adeline, anyway? I looked around, feeling pathetic. Maybe I should swim back to the dock. Maybe I should walk back to shore. Maybe I should hike back to Treble Cliff, put on my clothes, and pretend I'd never come here.

Suddenly there she was, pulling herself up the ladder and dripping her way over to me. "Hey, Melly. Sorry I'm late."

"It's okay. I was just . . . waiting." Now that Adeline was here, it was like in the movies, when the camera zooms in on just two people, and the rest of the crowd loses focus, their voices blurring and fading with their faces. We were in a bubble, there without being there.

"I didn't expect you to stand here doing nothing while you waited," she said, laughing.

"It's not that. It's just, they're having a diving contest. And, well, I can't." I shook my head, remembering the last time. "I tried at the Y, and it was a disaster. I got up on the diving board and had, like, heart-stopping, full-body paralysis."

Adeline nodded. "I get it. You're so high up, and you're supposed to just fall headfirst into the water?"

"Yes! Exactly."

"I hear you," she said. "You know, I could teach you to dive, if you'd let me. And there's no diving board to worry about."

My stomach twisted. At the thought of diving? At the thought of Adeline teaching me? "It's okay. This is your free time."

"Exactly. It's my free time. I can spend it how I want."

"But why would you want to spend it teaching me, when you could be having fun?"

"Who says it won't be fun?" Adeline said. "Melly, if you learn to dive today, then the rest of your time at Camp Rockaway, the rest of your life, you'll be able to dive whenever you want. You'll never have to say 'I can't dive' again. Please, trust me."

Didn't she get that it was myself I didn't trust? Adeline radiated confidence like sunshine. I was a black hole. I could suck up a million worries and have room for more.

Still, I didn't want to say no. "I trust you," I said. "Let's do it."

"Great!" Adeline's grin grew so wide it threatened to grab her ears. "But it's too wild on the raft. Let's swim back to the dock. I'll let the lifeguards know we need space for a lesson."

Over on the dock, Adeline made me sit on the edge, legs dangling in the water, while she positioned my arms. "Lean forward now," she said, pressing between my shoulder blades. "Farther—farther—"

Fear choked me. Suddenly I was leaning too far over the water to stay on the dock. *Plunk*—I fell into the water.

"You did it!" Adeline cheered as I came up sputtering. "Your first dive."

"That hardly counts." I pulled myself back onto the slippery white dock.

"Wrong. Every little step counts. You didn't learn to play drums in a day, did you? Now, ready to graduate to kneeling?" she said hopefully.

"Absolutely not."

I tried another sitting dive. My heart seized up as I leaned closer and closer to the water, but I realized something strangely good: the farther I leaned, the shorter the distance I had to fall.

I forgot to worry whether the other campers were watching. After every dive, Adeline gave me advice and asked if I was ready to try the next step. Eventually I felt ready to try a kneeling dive, and when I'd done okay with that, I agreed maybe I could try to dive standing up. Adeline showed me how to stand with my toes curled over the edge of the dock, my knees springy, my chin tucked. By now I felt confident enough to push off without prompting—

—and hit the water with a smack.

My body exploded with pain. The wind was knocked out of me. Tears stung my eyes. I hurt so much, I barely knew which way was up.

"Are you okay?" Adeline called.

I nodded, chin wobbling, and swam for the ladder. My thighs were covered with a bright red rash. How was it one moment your body could cut through the water like it was butter, and the next hit it like it was a brick wall?

"Take a breather," Adeline said. She disappeared down the dock and returned a minute later with her water bottle. She sat beside me and handed me the bottle. I took a grateful sip.

"You okay?" she asked again.

I nodded. My heart rate was returning to normal.

"Good. I know you're a percussionist, but maybe that was taking it a little too far."

It was a laugh-or-cry moment. I chose to laugh. "How was my sound?"

"A little flat." Adeline laughed with me. "You poor thing! That may be the worst belly flop I've ever seen."

"Don't you mean the best?" I said. "Give me some credit. That took talent."

"You're a natural," she agreed. "But you're supposed to be learning how to dive. Next time, try not to aim so far out. Deeper is better until you get more used to it."

"Next time?" I said in mock horror.

"You know you want to."

The crazy thing was I did.

"Come on," Adeline said, holding her hands out to me, "back on the horse."

"Great. You didn't tell me horses would be involved. You realize I've never ridden."

"You can save that adventure for another day. For now, imagine going to dinner and Olivia asking what you've done today. You can tell her you did a real dive."

I imagined doing just that. Would Olivia be proud? Jealous? Would she even care? I didn't know anymore. But I set down the water bottle and let Adeline help me up. "If I belly flop again, I'm done," I said.

I didn't, though. Adeline moved my arms and legs into position. I bent my knees, leaned forward, and aimed. I took one deep breath, then another. And when I was ready, I pushed off.

Water rushed past my ears, slid smoothly past my legs. I gave a few kicks underwater, then let myself drift back to the surface. When I emerged, it wasn't just Adeline cheering for me. It was the lifeguards. It was the kids on the raft. They were applauding as if I'd just finished playing the drum solo of my life.

Back on the dock, Adeline threw her arms around me and said, "I knew you could do it."

"It was still scary," I said. Even now, my knees were shaking.

Adeline held me by the shoulders. I felt a glow even warmer than the sun. "All the awesomest things are."

fourteen

That night we built a campfire in Treble Cliff, and I had my first honest-to-goodness s'more. The fire snapped and popped like a bowl of Rice Krispies. It filled the cool air with the scent of burning pine and sassafras. I patiently toasted my marshmallow until it was puffy and brown, ignoring Toni waving hers around like a torch. When she squished hers between her graham crackers, the insides burst through the charred skin, gooey and white, and when she bit down half of it ended up on her face. I laughed, until the same thing happened to me.

I guess some things are messy no matter what.

Olivia had been oddly quiet all evening. I'd have thought she'd be bubbling over from another afternoon spent with Noel, but instead she seemed distracted, staring into the dark spaces between the trees. It wasn't until the four of us were tucked into our tent that she said, "Shauna? Toni? Can I ask you a question?"

I felt a stab in my gut. What could she ask Shauna and Toni that she couldn't ask me? Then I realized how silly that sounded. When it came to Camp Rockaway, there were thousands of things Shauna and Toni knew better than I did.

"Go for it," Shauna told Olivia.

"It's about Sunday," she said.

"Sunday?" I interrupted.

"Field trip day," Toni said. "Second Sunday, we get in a van and go somewhere."

"Where?" We were in the middle of nowhere. Would it be one of those survival expeditions, where you got pushed out of a helicopter in the wilderness with nothing but a backpack and had to find your way back to camp?

"They like to keep it a surprise," Shauna said. "One year we went to Silver Lake and rode dune buggies. Another time it was speedboat rides on Grand Traverse Bay."

"One day of vacation, then back to the grind Monday morning," Toni said.

"Anyway," Olivia said, "I heard everyone's got to have a buddy. Someone they stick with for the entire day."

"Right," Shauna said. "Damon gets anxious about safety when we're off-site."

"So, what I'm wondering is do you think it would be weird if I asked Noel?"

A trapdoor opened inside me, and my stomach dropped through. Olivia and Noel—buddies? It was one thing for her to jam with him and his friends for a couple of hours every afternoon, but she was talking about spending a whole day with him, one on one. It was different. It was the kind of thing she should be doing with me.

Toni said, "You know, I had a hunch you were crushing on him!"

"Was it totally obvious?"

"There had to be some reason you'd spend all your free time playing—what was it?—the musical equivalent of stale bran muffins." Toni cackled.

"And now you want to be his field trip buddy," Shauna said. "That's intense. Not that you shouldn't do it. It's the twenty-first century. You want him to be your buddy, ask him."

"Question answered. It would be weird." Olivia groaned. "We hang out every day, but we're always playing music. I know how he plays. I want to get to know *him*."

"That makes sense," said Shauna. "And it wouldn't be weird, exactly. Most people buddy up with friends from their unit or their band, and Noel's in your band, so . . ."

"Besides, men like a bold woman," Toni said. "You want him, go get him!"

"What do you think, Melly?" Olivia asked. "Should I do it?"

"I don't know!" I said. I sounded whiny, and I hated it. But what was I supposed to say—*Sure, what's one more day at camp you'd rather spend with him than me*?

"I mean, will you be okay if I do?" she said. "Because if—"

"Yes!" I said, pulling my pillow over my head. "I'll be fine. Go ahead. Ask him."

"But who will be your buddy?"

"I'll find someone," I said. "I have other friends, you know."

"Right," Olivia said in an injured voice. "Of course. I didn't mean to imply you didn't."

"Maybe you could double-buddy," Shauna suggested. "Who's that other guy in your band, Olivia? If Melly buddies up with him, you'll still be together, and if things don't go well with Noel—"

"Not that she's saying they won't," Toni said.

"I'd never wish Brick on Melly," said Olivia.

"Or what about that boy in your band, Melly?" suggested Toni. "The quiet one, with the hair that's always in his eyes? He's cute."

"David?" I said incredulously. "I don't think he's said

— 146 —

a single word to me all week. Even if I wanted to ask him, there's no way he'd say yes. Seriously, everyone, I'll figure it out."

They left me alone after that, but I stayed awake and annoyed for a long time. Maybe I wasn't bold the way my friends were, but I wasn't helpless, either. Today I'd overcome my fear of diving. Who knew what I'd do next?

There had been a moment, earlier, when the campfire died low, barely more than embers. Blair had knelt and blown gently on them until flames once again licked over the wood. *That's me*, I thought. *There's something inside me, glowing, waiting to grow. It just needs a little air.*

Friday morning, Caleb brought charts for a song called "Pulse of the Maggots." Its title was enough to turn my stomach, but it turned out the song wasn't about literal fly larvae. The lyrics were a little confusing, but as near as I could figure, they were about standing strong and being true to yourself. The question was if anyone would be able to understand them through all the distortion and yelling. Listening to the recording Caleb had downloaded at the library, we walked through the same process as we had for every other song so far.

Donna must not have slept well. Now that we could

make it through our first four songs on our own, more or less, she sometimes let her guitar slump against the wall next to her, and she'd stop singing to listen to what we were doing. She praised our progress one moment and yelled at us to focus the next.

Finally she waved her arms in the air. "Stop, stop. For the love of Chuck Berry, stop."

We stopped. Our faces were flushed and frustrated, sweat beading our skin. David looked like a mop in need of wringing. Caleb's bushy blond hair stuck to his forehead. My own was matted against my neck. I envied Adeline her braids, but even she was fanning herself with her music folder.

"Listen," Donna said, "you've been playing together long enough that you're starting to get comfortable with each other. You're relaxing. That's good. But you're also getting lazy. You're not listening to each other."

She pushed open the door, and a blast of warm, muggy air entered the cabin. "Take five. Drink some water. Stretch your legs. Come back ready to focus. David and Melly—a word."

She tipped her head at us and frowned. My stomach flip-flopped. I imagined her telling me I was demoted to one of the little kids' bands. "Listen," she said. She touched us each on the shoulder. "Look up, okay? Eyes on me."

Bracing myself, I looked into her stern eyes. Beside

me, David slowly wiped his hair back behind his ears. "Now," Donna said, "look at each other."

David and I turned slowly toward each other. I found myself staring at the top of his head. His chin had dipped again. I wasn't sure if his eyes were on my chest or on my feet, but they definitely weren't on my face. When we were playing, I was sitting down and he stood beside me, so of course he was taller. Now I was taller by half a head.

"David!" Donna said. "Chin up. Eyes on Melly's. No, Melly, don't look away. This. This is your number one problem. You are both perfectly fine musicians. Keep practicing, and you'll get better and better. But that's an individual thing. What is holding you back as a band is communication. You two are the rhythm section. David, tell me the job of the rhythm section."

"To hold the beat down for the whole band," he muttered.

"Exactly. You're the foundation. You're the mortar. Everyone else depends on you to hold things together. But you can't do that if what, Melly?"

"If we don't communicate," I said. It was clearly what she wanted to hear.

"Right. Now is either of you a telepath? A mind reader? Obviously not, or we wouldn't be having problems. So tell me, how can you communicate?"

"With our eyes," I said, thinking of the signals I

shared with Olivia, "and faces."

"Or our hands," David said with a sigh.

"Or if all else fails, your voices," Donna said. "In a performance situation, if you need to say something to each other to prevent a train wreck, do it! Better a moment's distraction than a total disaster. Got it?"

We nodded.

"Okay. Lecture over. Now, as your instructor, it is my privilege to assign extra homework to students I think need it. Here's yours: I want you two to meet up every day outside of band practice. You don't have to play together, though of course that's not a terrible idea. But I want you to find a quiet place and practice making eye contact. Five minutes minimum."

"You want us to look each other in the eyes," David said. "For homework."

Donna frowned. "I really thought we were speaking the same language here."

"It sounds weird," I said. Actually, it sounded terrible.

"It will be weird," she said. "It will also make you a better rhythm section. And if I'm not mistaken, that's one of your goals at Camp Rockaway. Right or wrong?"

"Right," David and I mumbled.

"Great. Start today."

"Do you want us to report back to you?" I asked.

"No need," Donna said. "If you get better, I'll know you've been doing it. If you haven't—well, then maybe I'll have to sit in on your sessions."

Her words managed to sound immensely threatening. Donna bared her teeth in a sharklike smile. "I've used up your break. Go take one now. See you in five."

I grabbed my water bottle and left the cabin. If I hadn't needed a break before, I sure did now. Adeline was leaning against a tree. She waved to me, and I joined her.

"Can I be totally nosy and ask what Donna wanted with you and David?" she asked.

I sighed. "She wants us to stare at each other. To practice our communication skills."

Adeline looked at me like I was crazy, and I couldn't blame her. I kept a straight face for as long as I could. Then we both burst out laughing. "I know. It's bizarre."

"Yeah," said Adeline, "but so is the way David acts around you."

"Standoffish," I said. "That's the word my mom would use."

"I don't think it's that," she said. "Not on purpose, anyway. I think he's just shy."

"Well, it's not like I've ever given him a reason to be afraid of me."

"Except for being a girl."

"If he's terrified of half the world's population, he's not going to get very far in life."

"A cute girl," Adeline said. "A cute drummer girl."

"Ugh," I said. "Not you, too. Trust me, David and I are not going to happen."

"Then I shall never speak of it again."

"Do you really think I'm cute?" I blurted. Between the two of us, Olivia was always the one who got boys' attention. My parents told me I was beautiful, but that was the kind of thing parents did. I never actually believed them.

"Better than cute," Adeline said. "You're adorable."

Judging by the heat that suddenly rushed through my face, I turned approximately as red as a fire engine. Why had she said that? She didn't need to say that. "Adorable. Right."

"Don't let it go to your head. Nothing's less adorable than a big head." She winked.

I exhaled. Somehow it was easier—though a little disappointing, too—knowing she'd been kidding. "What about pus?" I asked. "Surely pus is even less adorable than a big head."

Adeline laughed. "Well, maybe a little."

"And what about raw sewage? What about ingrown hairs and toxic waste?"

"I take it all back. You are foul, disgusting, and definitely not adorable."

"Phew," I said. "Because seriously, I don't want David getting any ideas."

David and I met at the lodge after B-flat. He had his bass, and I had my sticks, to practice after we were done. Separately, of course. Heaven forbid we should play together if we didn't have to.

The stalls were the most private place we could think of. But I wished we'd chosen somewhere more public, even if other kids did look at us funny. The walls were too close. He was too close. And after what Adeline had said that morning, about David maybe liking me, I was feeling standoffish myself. "Let's get this over with," I said.

We sat cross-legged on the rug, and David shook back his hair. His face twisted uncomfortably. I suddenly wondered if doing this was as hard for him as diving had been for me. It seemed crazy, but maybe . . .

"Okay," I said, setting the timer on my watch. "On the count of three."

The first minute was terrible. Our eyes kept sliding away from each other. We'd catch ourselves and force our gazes back. David must have swept his hair from his eyes fifty times. It happened so much I started giggling. No wonder Donna was fed up with us. We were hopeless!

"Do you want a barrette or something?" I asked David.

"Do you have one?"

"No."

"A rubber band?"

"No. What about your bass strap?"

David opened his case, unhooked the embroidered strap from his bass, and tied it around his forehead. He looked like a hippie, and I laughed again. The tips of his ears turned dark.

"We're going to have to start over, you know," I said.

"Please don't say that," David said, crushing his hands against his face.

"I'm sorry," I said through my giggles, "but we have to. We really do."

That was why Donna's homework assignment was so evil. If we didn't do it, she wouldn't have to punish us. Our inevitable failure would be enough. I guess David realized the same thing. He started laughing, too. "Sorry. This is so awkward."

"I know," I said. "But we have to try."

It took two more false starts, but we finally got past our giggling. We stared at each other, chins propped in our hands. I found myself really noticing David's features for the first time. His eyes were very dark. They reminded me of Mom's morning coffee before she added cream and sugar. His eyebrows were black smudges. His nose bent just a little to the left. He had a couple of pimples, but who didn't? Toni was right, I realized. He was kind of cute.

I jumped when the timer on my watch beeped. David hopped up and unwound his bass strap from his forehead. His hair fell like curtains.

"See you at practice tomorrow," he mumbled.

"Yeah," I said. "See you." I backed out of the room, tripping over his amp as I went.

I didn't want to think about boys. Olivia, Toni, Adeline— why did everyone have to go there? Thanks to them, I was now wondering what it would be like to double-buddy with Olivia and Noel and David, when I knew it was a terrible idea. It was completely annoying.

At school, in those units on self-esteem, the ones that warn you about drugs and eating disorders and cutting yourself, they always tell you that if someone truly cares about you, they'll accept you for who you are. So why did everyone think they knew what was best for me? They weren't inside my head. They weren't inside my heart.

Get real. You're confused 95 percent of the time. No wonder you get pushed around.

I signed out a stall with a drum set and started

playing, forcing myself to go slow and easy. No particular song—I was free playing, following the beat wherever it led. I breathed in one measure, out the next, until my heart synced with my drums. The music unfurled inside me, expanding to fill every cranny of my brain and body, until there wasn't room left for anger or worry. It all melted away.

My arms and legs loosened up, and I began to play louder, faster. It was impossible to feel angry or helpless when I was in the groove. It was impossible to be a wallflower. I was in control here. I had the power. I would make the trees tremble for miles.

I kicked it up a notch, sweat gathering on the back of my neck, cymbals toppling wildly on their stands. I kicked it up another, and another, until—*crack*—a wild blow to the rim of a tom splintered one of my sticks in two.

Reality came crashing down around me. Control? Power? Only if I lived my entire life behind the drums. And apparently not even then. Growling, I left the stall, chucking the broken stick in the garbage.

The problem was I didn't know where to go next. I stormed to the Fretboard but didn't know where to flip my pick. I was standing there glowering when Adeline entered the clearing with her guitar. Ugh! Why couldn't she practice in the lodge like a normal person? Why did she have to show up, instead of a complete stranger? Someone who'd give me a funny look and let me go without saying a word?

She held out her hand. "Whoa, whoa, whoa. Melly, are you okay?"

I dodged away from her touch. "Yes. God. Why is everyone bothering me?"

Before she could answer, I ran back to the lodge. In the bathroom, I turned on the hot water and waited for it to warm up, but of course it didn't. I had to settle for splashing lukewarm water on my face, which I did until I wasn't completely blotchy and puffy.

I lifted my shirt to dry my face. All right. Tantrum over. Life would go on.

Outside, Adeline pushed herself off the stone wall of the lodge. "If you want me to go away, I will," she said. "But first, are you really okay?"

I sighed. "Yeah. Sorry for freaking out. It's been a weird day."

She nodded. "We don't have to talk about it unless you want to."

"I don't," I said. "But I wouldn't say no to canoeing. If you're not too busy." I'd been planning to go to another percussion workshop, but I needed a break from drums. And given what I'd done to that stick, maybe they needed a break from me.

"Nope, not too busy for canoeing," said Adeline. "Not with you, anyway. If Caleb asked me? Well, I might suddenly have other plans. Come on. Did you know there's a sunken rowboat in the lake? I'll show you."

This time when she reached out her hand, I didn't duck away. I took it.

fifteen

The sunken rowboat wasn't as exciting as it sounded. I could barely see it. I'd imagined pirate bones and a treasure chest spilling gold amid the cattails, which was silly, of course, considering we were on a tiny lake by a sheep farm in northern Michigan. Anyway, only when the light through the scudding clouds glinted just right could I see the dark, hulking shape of it.

Adeline pushed her paddle deep into the water and gave it a whack. It thudded dully. A cloud of minnows and sand whirled to the surface.

"How did it sink?" I asked.

"Don't tell me you've been at Camp Rockaway this long without hearing about Nessie Smith," Adeline said.

"Who?"

"She's smaller than the Loch Ness Monster, but she can still do some damage when she's got the blues. But don't worry. It's a well-known fact she only eats boys."

"Please don't say it's because she likes the flavor of testosterone," I said.

"Nope. Everyone has testosterone," Adeline said. "It's actually a mystery why she spares the girls. I guess she just likes them better."

There she was, teasing again. I heard it in her voice. But somehow it was never a mean kind of teasing. It was a kind that made me feel special, like she didn't bother joking around with just anyone.

Anyway, what *was* exciting was chatting with Adeline about everyday things as we paddled around the lake. Our favorite school subject (music, obviously). Our favorite movies (mine was *Little Women*, hers was *Pitch Perfect*). Our favorite books (mine was *Little Women* again, hers was *Brown Girl Dreaming*). I told her about Maki and asked if she had any pets.

"No pets," she said. "My parents say things are chaotic enough with three kids, and considering how crazy my brothers get, maybe they're right. But someday I'll adopt a whole bunch of dogs, every size and color. And I'll name them all after underappreciated musicians."

"Like who?" I asked.

"I could tell you, but you wouldn't have heard of them. Nobody's heard of them. That's the whole problem!"

Speaking of things I hadn't heard of, that reminded me of the stickers on her guitar case. "Hey, what does it mean, 'This machine kills fascists'?"

"Oh, the Woody Guthrie quote?" When I didn't respond, she said, "Melly! Please tell me you know who Woody Guthrie is. He's only one of the quintessential American folk singers of the twentieth century."

"Sorry," I said. "I don't know much about folk music."

"I guarantee you know one of his songs—This Land Is Your Land,'" Adeline said. "He was really political. During World War Two, he wrote a bunch of anti-fascist songs. Like, against dictatorships and stuff? He actually convinced the army to draft him as a musician instead of as a soldier because he believed it was the best way he could fight. And he had this sticker on his guitar—"

"'This machine kills fascists,'" I finished. "But with ideas, not bullets."

"Exactly!" Adeline said. "Awesome, right? I would love to write something influential someday. So far, most of my songs are pretty basic."

"You write songs?"

"Sometimes. I can't compose in the stalls—I feel completely boxed in—so I end up carrying my guitar all over camp to work on stuff. That thing I was humming the other day that you asked about? There's a reason you didn't recognize it. I was making it up."

"Oh. Wow." Was there anything Adeline wasn't good at?

"It's what I really want to do. I like singing and playing, but that's not my strength."

"What are you talking about?" I said, turning around. "You're an amazing musician."

Adeline gave me a look. "I'm not amazing. I'm fine. And I wasn't fishing for compliments. I'm just saying what I want to do isn't perform. I want to be more like Linda Perry."

"I've never heard of her."

"Yeah, she only had one big song of her own, and it was a long time ago. But I bet you've heard of Alicia Keys. Christina Aguilera. Gwen Stefani. Linda Perry wrote some of their biggest hits. I don't want the spotlight. I want to be the poet behind the scenes."

Hearing her say that somehow only made me like her more.

"Anyway, one thing's for sure," Adeline said. "Looks like I'm going to have to name one of my dogs Woody!"

After Adeline and I parted ways, the sky seemed to lose some of its blue. But she had to practice our songs, and we'd spent most of the afternoon together. I could hardly expect more.

In the short time I had before dinner, I swung past the craft cabin to pick up my maple seed key chain and got sucked into tie-dyeing a bandanna. I remembered how ridiculous David looked with the bass strap tied around his forehead, staring mournfully into my eyes, and laughed. That was when I knew I was truly feeling better: I could laugh again. I dyed a bandanna purple and orange to match David's purple Wyoming Junior High shirt and hung it on the line to dry. I could give it to him tomorrow.

Olivia grabbed her usual seat next to me at dinner. "He said yes!" she crowed.

"What?" I felt like I'd walked into the middle of the conversation.

"Noel." Olivia sounded disappointed I hadn't guessed. "About being buddies on Sunday."

"Oh, right. Great!" Dinner was tuna melts, and as I pulled a cheddar-oozing sandwich onto my plate I wondered what tonight's vegetarian option was. Adeline was sitting with Yasmina, which seemed to be where she always sat when she wasn't with us. They must have gotten really close over the years, to stay friends from summer to summer.

"Well?" Olivia said. "Don't you want to know what happened?"

"He said yes," I repeated stupidly.

"No! I mean, yes, I told you that, but *how* it happened." She rushed on. "I waited until after we were done playing, and Brick and Mikey had left, and I was like, 'Hey, you know the field trip?' And he was like, 'Yeah.' And I was like, 'Want to go with me?' And he was like, 'Me and some of the guys were planning to hang out. You can hang out with us.' And I was like, 'Cool, thanks, but do you want to go *with* me?' And he was like, 'Yeah, sure, why not?'"

As conversations went, it didn't sound very romantic to me. But what did I know? "I'm happy for you," I told Olivia.

"Thanks," she said. "Did you figure out your own buddy situation?"

Honestly, I hadn't even thought about it. "I've got plenty of time to figure it out," I said.

Just like that, her attention flipped back to Noel. "Hey," she said, turning to include the rest of the table, "do you think I should sit with Noel at firebowl? I mean, now that we're buddies, it wouldn't be a big deal, right?"

"Go ahead," I said. I knew she wouldn't hear any other answer.

"Just realize Toni's going to make you tell us all about it later," said Shauna.

"That's right," Toni said. "The lights go off, and the truth comes out!"

"Okay," Olivia said, breathing deeply. "I'll do it."

That's when I noticed that even though most of the table was cheering Olivia on, Candace's face was tight, her mouth small. I had a feeling this whole thing might turn out to be a bigger deal than Olivia thought—and not in a good way.

At firebowl, Olivia waved good-bye and went to find Noel. Adeline motioned the rest of us over to the bench she was sharing with Yasmina. I slid onto the log beside her. Toni and Shauna followed, and Damon started firebowl with a sing-along of "Sloop John B." The music mingling with the hisses and pops of the bonfire reminded me of the scratchy old record player at Grandma Goodwin's house.

I still wasn't ready to join the song leaders in front of the crowd, but that didn't bother me. Listening and singing and tapping my toes on the pine-needled earth was plenty.

Since the afternoon, the clouds had piled up on each other over the lake and trees. It seemed like you could poke the air with a pin, and water would stream out through the tiny hole. Adeline said, "Bet it'll rain tonight."

"Yeah?"

"Nothing beats a midnight rainstorm at Camp Rockaway. The sound of the rain through the leaves, pattering on the roof of your tent. And thunder so loud the ground shakes. Fun fact—did you know a lake attracts lightning like a magnet?"

My skin prickled as if static were already building

around us. My hair stood on end. I had that increasingly familiar sensation of knowing exactly how much distance was between me and Adeline at every moment, felt a tug every time one of us shifted on the log. My head started to do the floaty balloon thing. I shut my eyes and hugged myself tight.

Stay here. Stay on the ground.

"Are you cold?" Adeline whispered.

I realized with surprise that I was shivering. "A little," I said.

"Here. My sweatshirt's enormous. We can share."

She unzipped her hoodie and draped it across our shoulders—and *zap*. With my left side pressed up against Adeline, the tension in the air became an electrical current shooting between our arms where they touched, between our hips and knees. I looked at Adeline out of the corner of my eye, to see if she felt it, too, but she stared straight ahead, down at the fire, singing as if nothing out of the ordinary were happening.

Then the first drops of rain spilled from the sky, sending puffs of steam hissing into the air from the coals. The music stopped immediately. Around us campers shrieked and covered their heads. "Calm down!" Damon called. "It's only a little water."

But the rain pelted harder, and it was clear firebowl was over. The counselors did their best to herd us back to our campsites in a semi-orderly fashion so we could grab our toothbrushes and take care of bedtime preparations before the storm really hit. In the commotion, I lost track of Adeline.

I was drenched by the time we made it back to our tents for good. We laid our soaked, mud-streaked socks on the floor to dry out. It smelled awful, but we couldn't put them in our laundry bags without ruining everything else. By the time we climbed into bed, our tent flaps tied firmly against the wind and rain, the entire floor was covered with wet clothing.

With our flashlights off, darkness folded around me, I felt curled inside a drum. The rain beat down on the canvas roof in flams and paradiddles. I snuggled deep inside my sleeping bag. My pillow was moist from the humidity, but I didn't care. Adeline was right: this was terrific.

I wondered if my parents were watching the weather report and worrying about me sleeping in a tent in the woods in this deluge. I sort of hoped they were. Then I remembered Dad still hadn't written me a letter. He probably hadn't given one thought to me. I felt sick at that.

But there was nothing I could do. Nothing but close my eyes and let the rain pound and puddle in my brain so I didn't have to think anymore.

sixteen

It was still raining hard when Poppy gave the morning wake-up call. During the night I'd been yanked from sleep over and over as thunder crackled and boomed. I was really too old to be afraid of a thunderstorm, but it freaked me out a little not to have solid walls and a solid roof between me and the weather. I imagined lightning splitting a tree and sending it toppling onto our tent, crushing all four of us. After that I barely slept at all.

Across the tent, Shauna groaned loudly. I turned on my flashlight. All I could see of her was a few curls. The rest of her was scrunched into her sleeping bag like a neon green caterpillar. Toni didn't even stir.

"Hey, Olivia," I whispered.

"Why are you whispering?" Olivia said groggily.

"That's a great question," I whispered back.

Shauna sat bolt upright and belted, "'Oh, what a beautiful mornin'! Oh, what a beautiful day!'"

Olivia clamped her pillow over her head. "Make it stop, please."

Toni woke with a start. "What's going on? Is there a tornado? Do we have to evacuate?"

I burst out laughing. I rolled out of bed, kicked my damp, dirty clothes out of the way, and peeled back a tent flap to let in some light. It didn't look like daytime outside. The sky was the color of steel. The pine trees glistened, tiny pearls of rainwater clinging to their needles. A metallic smell hung in the air.

"Oh God, my feet are soaked!" Olivia yelled. She kicked off her sleeping bag and ducked out from under her mosquito netting to investigate. "There's a leak! This whole corner is drenched!"

Toni joined her. "Oopsy-daisy. Somebody didn't lace up her corner of the tent."

"Sure, let's blame *somebody* who's never been in the woods before, much less camped in the middle of freaking nowhere in a giant freaking canvas lunch sack. How was I supposed to know?" Olivia sounded close to tears.

"Hey," I said, "it wasn't your fault. We'll fix this, okay? What got wet?"

Olivia grumpily poked around and discovered the only casualty was the end of her sleeping bag. She'd slept curled up, her knees tucked to her chest, so it wasn't until this morning that she'd stretched her legs and her toes ended up in the cold, soggy spot.

"Maybe there's a dryer Poppy can put it in," I said, faking confidence. "Anyway, I bet it'll dry out by tonight."

We put on our rain ponchos and gathered in the fire circle to go to breakfast. It turned out several people had wet sleeping bags. "Not to worry. We'll hang them up when the sun comes out," Poppy said cheerfully.

"Sure. When'll that be?" Olivia muttered.

"'Tomorrow,'" Shauna said, breaking into song again, "'tomorrow, I love ya, tomorrow!'"

"Gah," Olivia said. "Enough, already!"

"Buck up, women," Blair said. "Camp doesn't stop for rain. You've got band practice to go to. Everything but the beach and the meadow will be open all day. Regularly scheduled workshops will go on. And in the lodge—"

"Movie Musical Marathon!" Shauna squealed.

That explained the show tunes.

"Much as it pains me, yes: Camp Rockaway's traditional rainy-day Movie Musical Marathon. Bring your pillow to the lodge, and rot your brains as long as you like. Hot beverages will be available. We'll be using the TV from the library, so anyone who set aside today to watch instructional videos and actually learn something useful, sorry, you're out of luck."

"What's showing?" Candace asked.

"*Camp Rock,* naturally," Blair said. "On repeat."

"I really, really hope she's kidding," said Olivia.

I don't know if our first staring practice helped David and me communicate any better. But the bandanna I'd tie-dyed sure did. It hadn't completely dried by the time I picked it up after breakfast, but then, nothing was dry at this point. "Here," I said, handing it to him as we stripped off our wet ponchos in Trolltunga. "This is for you."

"What is it?" he asked.

"I figured you'd need your bass strap for actually playing bass," I said.

A smile flickered across his face—what I could see of it, anyway. "Thanks." He tied it around his head, his hair tucked behind his ears. I could see his whole smile then. It was nice.

Donna said nothing but nodded approvingly. She didn't stop practice once to tell us to *focus* and *communicate.* I guess we'd passed our first day's homework. A few minutes before our session was supposed to end, though, she said, "People, we need to talk."

We all looked at each other. Our playing had drowned out the rain. Now I heard it tapping lightly on the roof, as well as the faint sound of drums and bass from the other cabins in the clearing. What was Donna going to say?

"Jeez, it's nothing to worry about," she said. "We need to take stock and look ahead to next week. You have tomorrow off because of the field trip, which means you need to come back doubly focused on Monday. Who wants to remind me what's one week from today?"

"The final show," Adeline said. "For all of camp, plus all our families."

"The four of you will be on stage in front of, quite literally, hundreds of people. Maybe you're used to that. Maybe it's your first time. Either way, you need to be ready." Donna turned an evaluating, half-lidded stare on each of us. "We spent our first week getting used to playing together and starting to learn the music. Next week, we'll solidify our relationship with each other, finish arranging and memorizing the songs on our set list, and work on stage skills."

"What's even on our set list?" Caleb asked.

"Brilliant question. Yes. What's on your set list? That's one of the things you will need to start discussing right now. You have ten minutes on that stage, counting plugging and unplugging. That can be three radio hits or one 'Stairway to Heaven.' It's your call. You'll also need to come up with a band name."

"What," Adeline joked, "we can't be anonymous?"

"Knock yourselves out," said Donna. "This is me, removing myself from the conversation in three, two—" She pointed her index fingers at us and backed out of the circle. She grabbed an issue of *Vive Le Rock!* out of her messenger bag and slid to the floor to read it.

"So," Adeline said.

"So," Caleb and I said.

David looked at his feet. I got the feeling he wanted to take off the bandanna and let his hair cover his face again.

"I think we should do 'Pulse of the Maggots,'" Caleb said. "It rocks the hardest."

"It may rock," Adeline said, "but we don't. That's our weakest. We barely know it!"

"Speak for yourself," said Caleb. "I've got that guitar solo nailed."

"It kills my voice every time. Not to mention I feel ridiculous playing acoustic on it."

"Don't get mad at me because of your shortcomings."

"Please stop," I said. "We've got other songs we can do."

"Like Taylor Swift. Great." Caleb chirped, "'I knew you were trouble . . .'" I waited for Donna to warn us about being respectful, but she ignored us. We were on our own.

"Have you paid any attention to the lyrics of that

song?" said Adeline. "It's about how a dysfunctional relationship can completely destroy you. Think: the part about drowning. The part about lying on the cold, hard ground. Maybe it's about love, but it isn't lovey-dovey."

"Right," Caleb said, rolling his eyes. "And that's why girls—"

"Caleb, wait," I said. "I think Adeline's right."

His eyes widened. He must not have expected me to have an opinion.

"At first it sounds like just another happy pop song. But the lyrics are actually really angsty," I said. "It's like if you had, I don't know, a piece of roadkill. You could wrap it up with a pretty bow, but it would still be a piece of roadkill."

Everyone stared at me like I'd teleported into Trolltunga from another planet. Then Caleb picked up his guitar. He started playing fast and hard. The song sounded familiar, but I couldn't place it. David asked the question in everyone's mind: "What is that?"

"You don't recognize it?" Caleb said. A wild, crooked smile came over his face, and the pieces of the puzzle snapped into place. I laughed. Of everyone in the room, only Caleb had understood my roadkill metaphor. It figured.

"What's so funny?" said Adeline.

"It's still Taylor Swift," I said. "He just changed the packaging."

"Gave it some improvements," said Caleb.

I wasn't sure speeding up the song and adding a bunch of discordant licks and distortion were improvements. But it was different. Interesting. My bandmates stared in bewilderment and awe as Caleb snarled, "'Trouble, trouble, trouble.'"

"Hey," Adeline said, "what if we did the same thing with 'Enter Sandman'?"

Caleb's fingers literally screeched to a halt. "Uh, hello. It's already a metal song."

"I mean taking it the opposite direction. Turning it into a pop song."

"No! If you want to mess with Metallica, do it on your own time. I refuse to be part of it."

"Okay, okay. But since it's basically a creepy lullaby already—all that stuff about sleeping with one eye open and gripping your pillow tight—what about this?"

Adeline picked up her guitar and began playing the chorus of "Enter Sandman" at a fraction of the usual tempo, keeping a light touch on the strings. She sang with none of the original's rage. Instead her voice was a moan, a quaver, eerie and haunting. If Metallica's version was a band of demons playing in your bedroom closet, Adeline's was the trees scratching your bedroom windows in the middle of the night. It sent a shiver down my spine.

"That sounded like 'Rock-a-bye Baby' sung by a

dead person," Caleb said.

"I couldn't have put it better myself," Adeline said smugly.

"I like it," I said. "David?"

He nodded. "As long as we keep the bass line. I feel like I just got it."

"Of course," said Adeline.

"Fantastic," Donna said, and we jumped. She rejoined our circle. "Sorry to cut you off, but we're out of time. I liked what I heard. Listen, people. Remember one of your goals is to develop your sound as a group. This is a great beginning. Come back Monday ready to rock some new arrangements."

It was the most approval she'd given us all week. The four of us actually looked at each other and smiled. Adeline leaned forward, eyes sparkling. "Melly? Caleb? David? We are going to kill it next week."

seventeen

The rain alternated between downpour and drizzle all morning, but it never stopped completely. My poncho didn't cover much below the knees, so my shoes and socks got soaked all over again. After lunch, I pulled out a fresh pair of socks and discovered everything in my suitcase was clammy.

"What do you think?" I asked Olivia. "Want to watch a movie after B-flat?"

I'm not sure why I asked. She said exactly what I thought she'd say. "I was going to jam with Noel. You don't mind, do you?"

"When have I ever?"

Olivia was too distracted to notice my sarcasm. "Thanks, Melly, you're the best."

Was she even listening? What had happened to the Olivia who'd called me the second she heard my parents were getting divorced, who'd offered to come over so I wouldn't be alone on the worst day of my life? What had happened to the friend and musical partner who'd begged Damon to put us in a band together? One week later, she barely seemed to remember I existed.

Olivia or no Olivia, I was determined to have a good afternoon. Unfortunately, I was thinking in sunny day terms, when I could do whatever I wanted whenever I wanted. David and I got staring practice out of the way quickly, but because of the rain, the stalls were swamped with campers. There wasn't a stall with a drum set available until almost dinnertime. I should've signed up for one right after breakfast. I checked to see if there was a percussion workshop scheduled, but I was out of luck. There was nothing to look forward to but hours of rain—and a bunch of movies I didn't want to watch.

I hung in the back of the lodge long enough to get a cup of hot chocolate and see that the movie on TV was *A Hard Day's Night*, a comedy starring the Beatles. They sang their way through ridiculous situations that would never happen to rock stars in real life. If I'd had a friend to watch it with, I might have found it funny. Instead, I was immediately bored.

Where was Adeline? Not here in the lodge—I'd scanned the crowd and would've recognized her even in the dim light. I didn't see Yasmina either. Maybe the two of them were hanging out somewhere together. Or maybe she'd nabbed a practice stall, even though she said she didn't like them.

I imagined wandering around in the rain looking for her, but that seemed sort of pathetic. What did I want from Adeline, anyway? Why was she the person, more than Shauna or Toni or even Olivia, my mind always seemed to turn to when I was feeling lonely or bored—and sometimes, too, when I wasn't thinking of anything at all?

Okay, she'd been nice to me. She was nice to everyone, except maybe Caleb, but I was pretty sure she was extra nice to me. She'd been there for me when I was ready to melt down. She'd seen me cry twice, for crying out loud, and hadn't been scared off. But her being *nice* didn't explain why I didn't even have to close my eyes to conjure her bright brown eyes or her grin flashing with braces. It didn't explain the rustling leaves in my stomach or my heart full of bees.

The Beatles burst into "All My Loving," and I shook my head.

I turned from the TV, put my dripping poncho back on, and reentered the rain. It was barely sprinkling, the sky was lightening, and for a moment I was hopeful the lifeguards would reopen the beach. I could practice my diving, or maybe take out one of the little red kayaks. After all the new things I'd tried this week, I was sure I could manage one. But before I'd gone far there came another murmur of thunder. There went that idea.

I was on my way back to the Fretboard, unsure where to go next, when I realized how stupid I'd been. I didn't have to wonder where Adeline was. I could look for the pick with her name on it! I stood in the rain, getting soaked all over again as I searched.

She wasn't in the stalls or Treble Cliff. Not at the crafts cabin or the nature cabin, either. Then I caught a glimpse of "A-D-E," and before I got to "L-I-N-E," my wet, muddy shoes had sprouted wings. I flipped my pick and ran for the library.

It was bigger than most of the other cabins. The front room housed instruments you could borrow and a wall of filing cabinets full of charts, organized by recording artist. There was a copy machine and a computer the counselors could use to download charts and recordings if they didn't already have the one you wanted. On the corner of the desk were piles of staff paper and tab paper so you could write your own.

The back room had bookcases full of books, videos, music, and the stereo equipment to play it on. Campers lounged on threadbare sofas and beanbag chairs. There was an empty spot in the corner, which I guessed was where the TV belonged.

Adeline was nowhere to be seen.

"Anything I can help you with?" a counselor asked, coming up behind me as I traced my fingers along the spines of the books. "Looking for a little inspiration?"

I felt gross and wet and heavy all over again. I must have just missed Adeline. She must have been here until a couple of minutes ago, and somehow we'd crossed paths. Maybe there was more than one trail between here and the Fretboard. She could be anywhere by now.

Go back and check her pick again, one part of me urged.

No. You can't chase her all over camp. That's beyond sad. Get a life, Melly!

"I guess I have cabin fever," I said, trying to hide my disappointment.

Armani—that was his name, I remembered—nodded. "I get it. You spend so much time cooped up at home, or at school. It doesn't seem right for it to happen here, too. Tell you what. Why don't you try the balcony?"

"Balcony?" I pictured the library's outside and realized that yes, it did have another story. But I hadn't seen a balcony, only windows.

"It's in the back, facing into the trees. Not much of a view even on the best of days, unless you're into bird-watching. But it's a nice, quiet place to get some fresh air. We try not to advertise it to campers, since you have to cut through the attic, which is kind of a disaster area. But I can trust you not to shout it around, can't I?"

I nodded. Armani pointed to the door behind the staff desk. I grabbed a random book from the shelf to justify my presence in the library. It wasn't until I was halfway up the stairs that I looked at the cover: *Music Fundamentals and Functional Skills*. Ugh.

Upstairs, the roof slanted sharply on either side. The attic was crowded with boxes and filing cabinets, which I guessed were full of more charts. It smelled of old paper and wood. I crossed the room to the door at the far end. Watery gray-green light spilled through the window. Rain streamed endlessly from the eaves.

But my whole field of vision lit up when I stepped onto the balcony and saw Adeline.

She blinked up at me from the glider, a notebook open on her knees, pen in hand. "Hey. How did you find me?"

I shook my head, almost too surprised to be happy. "I . . . I wasn't looking for you. I mean, I *was* . . . but I gave up because I thought . . . and then I came up here to get some air."

"Wow," Adeline said. "Weird. Guess it was meant to be. Want to sit?"

She gestured at the empty half of the glider. The only other seat was a mildewed deck chair. Adeline had draped her poncho over the back of it. I took off my poncho, too, and sat beside her. The glider squeaked each time it rocked forward and sighed each time it rocked back.

Adeline eyed the book in my lap. "What, no more Sheila E.?"

"She's back in Treble Cliff."

"So you thought you'd go for a little light reading. How is it?"

"Well, it's . . ." I searched for an answer that wouldn't make me sound like a dunce who didn't even know what functional skills were. Then I remembered this was Adeline. She didn't need a made-up answer. "I have no idea. I picked it up by accident. It looks like the most boring book ever written."

"I'm glad you said it," Adeline said, "because I was sure thinking it."

We laughed and settled into a comfortable silence.

"It's beautiful, isn't it?" she said. "The rain."

I didn't answer right away. The truth was more complicated than a simple yes or no.

She said, "Camp goes by so fast sometimes. When it rains, everything has to slow down. I get to think about the stuff that's already happened. Catch my breath before it all starts again."

"I could do without the wet socks," I said. "My feet are like giant prunes."

"Take them off. That's what I did."

Sure enough, Adeline's feet were bare, her brown toes flexing against the flaking green paint on the balcony. She'd tossed her shoes into the corner. I followed her example. My feet were pale and wrinkled.

"Ugh. They look like they've been living underground," I said. "Like naked mole rats."

"Poetic," Adeline said, and I giggled.

"Are you working on a song?" I asked.

"Trying to."

"I'll shut up. I'll let you write."

"And you'll read that horrible book?" Adeline said. We laughed again. "I'm ready for a break anyway. The notebook's here in case I think of something absolutely ingenious to write."

She set both notebook and pen on the floor beside the glider and put out her hand for my book. I handed it to her. Adeline pulled back her arm as if to hurl it off the balcony into the trees, but at the last second she set it on the floor with the other things. "There," she said.

"I guess the rain is sort of beautiful," I admitted. "It makes everything extra green. It's different back home. The buildings and roads get even grayer than normal. And the water feels clean when it's falling, but then it stirs up all the oil and crud on the ground."

"That's true," said Adeline. "Though I like that,

too—not the crud, but the little rainbow swirls on top of the puddles. You're right about the colors being more intense. I picture Marquette in the rain, all its old red brick buildings hanging over the harbor. It's like someone took a photo of it in the sunshine and ran it through a color copier, the way the colors get deeper and darker."

"You know what I love?" I said. "Riding in a car in the rain at night. All dry and warm while the rain drums on the roof and leaves streaks on the windows. And the lights —the streetlights and the headlights— they're burning all around, like stars, reflected in the windows and puddles. It makes me feel like I'm flying through outer space or something."

I stopped. Adeline was staring at me.

"Sorry," I said. "I'm not usually such a blabbermouth."

She shook her head. "Naked mole rat feet aside, you really are a poet."

"No, trust me, if I say anything remotely poetic, it's a fluke. I wouldn't know how to begin writing a song."

"You could go to a songwriting workshop," she said. "It's lots of fun."

"I don't think so. I wouldn't even know what to write about."

"That's the beauty of it. You can write a song about literally anything. Yellow submarines. Oscar Mayer wieners. Little red Corvettes. The circle of life."

I rolled my eyes. "Pruny feet."

"You could!" said Adeline. "But what you said, about driving in the rain at night—that is song-worthy, my friend."

"No. I couldn't just make up something. I know I couldn't."

"You do it all the time," she argued. "You're a musician. You create music."

I shook my head. "Drummers support. They don't lead. They don't write songs."

"That's ridiculous. What about Don Henley? Neil Peart? Your old friend Sheila E.?"

"Fine. *I* don't lead. *I* don't make songs materialize out of thin air."

"It's not so much materializing as digging a hole to China with a teaspoon," Adeline said.

"Because that sounds like so much fun," I said. But a smile tugged at the corner of my mouth.

"Except when it's pure magic and it really does seem to come out of thin air. Like a line about street-lights becoming colored stars. That's amazing, Melly," she said in a coaxing voice.

"Tell you what," I said. "You think it's so amazing? It's yours, no strings attached."

Adeline didn't answer. Instead she stood and

stretched, draping herself over the railing. She squinted up at the sky. "I can't tell if it's still raining or if it's just dripping from the trees."

"I haven't heard thunder in a while," I said.

"Me neither. I almost hope it keeps raining a while longer, though."

"Why?" I asked.

"Like I said." Adeline settled back onto the glider. Maybe it was my imagination, but I thought she sat a little closer than before. "I don't want camp to go by too fast."

Right then, neither did I.

eighteen

The rain cleared up by the end of dinner. Blair and Poppy strung clotheslines between the trees in Treble Cliff. Everyone clamored for space. A lot of us ended up hanging our dirty socks on random evergreen branches. "Ugliest Christmas trees ever," Toni said, and I had to agree.

All week I'd heard murmurs of a dance party Saturday night, but now that the time had come, the murmurs became a roar. If preparations for the open mic were excruciating, they were nothing compared to this.

"Why didn't I bring a dress?" Olivia moaned as she rifled through her suitcase, flinging clothing behind her like a puppy digging for a bone. "Or at least a skirt?"

I didn't say anything because what could I say? Even if I had a magic wand to *poof* the perfect outfit into existence, I had the feeling it wouldn't make Olivia any less anxious. It wasn't until coming to camp that I realized how much I normally depended on Olivia to be cool and confident. Back home, she made it so easy to follow her lead. I was happy to play backup for her. But here, where she should've been in her element, surrounded by musicians as passionate as she was, she seemed completely off her game. And it turned out Olivia-off-her-game was not fun to deal with. Our roles were reversed, with one small problem: I didn't know how to lead.

As she sulkily settled for jeans and a T-shirt with a silver star on it, I said the only thing I could say. "You look great."

Shauna wore a Western shirt with pearly snap-together buttons, jeans, and cowboy boots. I waited for a cowboy—excuse me, *cow woman*—hat to pop from her suitcase, but instead she French braided her hair into two thick pigtails.

Toni wore a shirt with a stick figure holding a microphone. Olivia squinted to read it. "'I'm big in . . . big in . . .'"

"'I'm big in Lilliput,'" Toni said.

Shauna burst into laughter. "Toni, are you sure you want to wear that shirt to the dance?"

Olivia raised an eyebrow. "Why wouldn't she?"

"Yeah, Shauna," Toni said. "Why wouldn't I? It's a city in Norway. It's like saying, 'I'm big in Japan.'"

Shauna wiped tears from her eyes. "No, no, no. Lilliput is not in Norway," she said. "It's a made-up place from this old book *Gulliver's Travels*. The people there are all one inch tall."

"Possibly the only place in the world Toni would qualify as big," I said with a giggle.

Toni sighed. "That explains why my dad had such a goofy look on his face when he gave it to me. Stupid English teacher humor."

"Do you want me to see if I have something else you can wear?" Shauna asked. "You could probably wear one of my shirts as a tunic."

"Nope," Toni said. "I may only be four foot, eight inches, but all the more reason I've got to stand by every one of them. Now, where's my glitter?"

I settled for clean jeans and a relatively unwrinkled T-shirt with two drumsticks that said, "This is how I roll." Cheesy, but at least I'd been in on the joke from the beginning.

"Ugh, my stomach is Butterfly City." Olivia moaned. "I'm going to barf. And if I barf, I can't dance. And if I don't dance, there is absolutely no way Noel is going to kiss me."

"Is he going to kiss you?" I asked, startled.

"I don't know! Maybe."

I couldn't explain why the possibility was alarming, but it was. Did I think once she kissed Noel, I'd somehow lose her for good? That was silly. They could spend the next week glued to each other, but she'd have to come home with me at the end.

Still, this week the ground had splintered between us. I hoped once we returned home, the cracks would seal up. But what if Olivia kissing Noel widened them into a canyon that couldn't be crossed?

"Just don't barf when he kisses you," Toni said, "and you'll be good."

The dining tables had been cleared from the floor of the lodge. The overhead lights were off. Drums and guitars glinted in the stage lights. The windows were open, and the funky smell of wet ponchos and soggy sneakers had begun to fade. Damon and his posse ran up onstage and started their set with "Livin' la Vida Loca." Everyone began bouncing.

In many ways, it was just like our first night at Camp Rockaway. The same place, the same people, the same kind of upbeat music. There was one key difference: this time I wasn't nervous. My friends drew me into the melee, Shauna stomping and clapping, Toni bopping around like she was on a pogo stick, Olivia twirling and whirling like a dandelion seed on the wind. I felt dizzy in the best possible way.

When Olivia leaned in to my ear and said, "I'm going to try to find Noel," I was neither surprised nor disappointed. Because there were Adeline and Candace and the rest of Treble Cliff. There were Blair and Poppy and the rest of our counselors. There was a whole group of little kids starting a conga line. I wasn't alone. I was the furthest thing from it.

The evening flew by. It didn't seem right when Damon announced, "Time to slow things down."

The band plunged into the gentle reggae beat of "Three Little Birds." You couldn't have cleared the dance floor faster if you'd set off a stink bomb. Most kids ran for the punch bowl, but some of the older campers trickled back in, pairing up. I leaned against the wall and watched. I didn't feel bad that I didn't have anyone to dance with. It was enough to enjoy the music.

"Hey." Adeline leaned against the wall beside me.

"Hey," I said. "Where's Yasmina?"

"Out there." Adeline nodded at the dance floor.

"Ah. Yeah. Olivia, too." I could just make out her dark hair against the white of Noel's shirt as they spun slowly around.

"We could go out there," said Adeline teasingly. "If you wanted."

I couldn't tell if she was serious. All the couples on

the dance floor were boy-girl, except for some little kids who were mocking the whole thing, and a pair of high school boys who were clearly boyfriend and boyfriend, at least for camp. It was one thing to dance the fast songs with your girl friends. Slow songs were something else. I didn't know how to slow dance anyway.

"I don't think so," I said, trying to match her light tone. "You're wearing sandals, and I'd step all over your toes. Seriously, it's for your own good."

She shrugged. "That's okay. I'm worn out, anyway."

As the band segued into another slow song, Adeline slid to the floor and pulled me down next to her. Even when I was sitting beside her, she didn't let go of my hand.

"Hey," I said, pretending my heart wasn't threatening to rocket from my chest, "I heard we need a buddy for the field trip tomorrow. Do you have one yet?"

"I don't," she said, shifting her fingers for a more comfortable grip. "Do you?"

"No. I thought you might be partners with Yasmina."

"And I thought you might be partners with Olivia."

"She's going with Noel," I said.

"Ah," Adeline said. "They're getting pretty serious, huh?"

"Apparently. She's liked boys before, but nothing this bad."

"Camp'll do that."

We watched the dancing couples, through one whole song and then another. They held each other as if they were glass. I imagined I could see inside them, to their pulses fluttering like red moths. They rocked side to side, awkwardly orbiting each other, seemingly unaware that anyone was watching. Could I ever be that brave?

As Damon announced the final song, Olivia hurried over. Right away I let go of Adeline's hand. I felt like I'd been caught doing something . . . not *wrong*, exactly, but weird. Weird for me, anyway. Other girls held hands sometimes, and it was no big deal. But that was them. I didn't come from a touchy-feely family. Olivia and I had never been touchy-feely friends.

"Melly, have you seen Noel?" Olivia asked.

I shook my head. "I thought you were with him."

"I was, until he said he had to go to the bathroom. But it's been, like, ten minutes, and he hasn't come back. I can't find him anywhere! Help me look. Please."

I stood. "I'm sure he's somewhere. Come on." To Adeline I said shyly, "See you later?"

Adeline nodded. "Tomorrow."

My own little moth burst into flames.

Olivia and I wove between the couples on the dance floor. We split up and paced the perimeter in opposite directions. The last notes died away, and the fluorescent lights flicked on in one jarring moment that left everyone blinking. Noel wasn't anywhere.

It wasn't until the counselors had rounded up everyone, lining us up in our units to return to our campsites, that he skulked back into the lodge from outside with a couple of other boys. As soon as she saw him, Olivia splintered from our group, but Poppy called, "Olivia, over here, please." She had to return with her questions unanswered.

"Why would he do that?" she asked as we hiked to Treble Cliff. "Why would he leave, when he knew I was waiting for him?"

"Maybe the dance ended sooner than he was expecting. Maybe he missed the announcement about the last song."

"Maybe. Argh! Now I'm going to be awake all night worrying he's mad at me."

I shook my head. "Why would he be mad at you?"

"I don't know. But if he was happy, he wouldn't have lied, would he? He said he was going to the bathroom, but he came in from outside! He wasn't even in the lodge." Her voice spiraled up and up.

"Tomorrow's the field trip," I said. "You'll get to spend the whole day with him. It'll be great. Just wait and see."

Olivia looked like she didn't believe me. I couldn't blame her one bit.

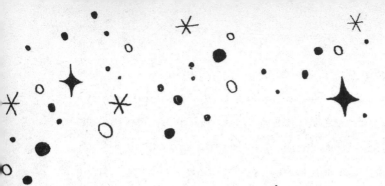

nineteen

We woke the next morning to a knock at our tent pole and Poppy saying, "Up and at 'em!" Toni groaned, which Poppy took as an invitation to pull back a flap. Sunshine poured in. Toni shrieked like a vampire in daylight and burrowed deeper into her sleeping bag.

"Put on your swimsuit under your clothes, and grab your beach towel," Poppy said.

Shauna sat up. "Are we going to Lake Michigan? Are we going to Sleeping Bear Dunes?"

Blair walked up behind Poppy, yawning loudly. "You'll never find out if you don't get out of bed in the next ten seconds. The vans are leaving at eight o'clock sharp, whether or not we're on them."

"What about breakfast?" I asked. Any extra energy I'd gotten from last night's punch and cookies, I'd burned off dancing.

"'What about coffee?' would be a better question," Blair said.

"We'll eat on the road," said Poppy. "Now hop up! We've got a big day ahead." Our counselors turned and left to rouse the next tent.

There were bags under Olivia's eyes. "I feel horrible," she whispered as she crawled out of bed, clutching her stomach.

"Horrible like you need to go to the infirmary?" I asked. "Is it your period? I bet they have Aleve."

"No. Horrible from last night."

I tried not to sigh. "It's going to be fine. You'll find Noel when we get down to the parking lot. I'm sure last night was just a misunderstanding." There was only so worried I could feel on Olivia's behalf. I was going to spend the entire day with Adeline! I couldn't wait.

Towels draped over our arms and around our shoulders, we marched to the parking lot. It was the first time I'd set foot in it since arriving at camp. It was weird being back. I felt a pang. I wasn't ready to leave. But instead of my mother's car and dozens of SUVs and minivans filling the space, there was a fleet of rental vans. I relaxed, satisfied we weren't leaving for good.

When all the units were assembled, Damon called for everyone's attention. "Okay, rock stars. Today, you're going on an adventure outside of camp. Think of it as an opportunity to recharge your creative batteries."

Everyone cheered. Adeline caught my eye, and we shared a smile. I remembered holding hands with her the night before, and my heartbeat kicked up a notch.

"A couple of safety things before we head out. As you probably know, everyone must have a buddy for the entire day. If something happens to you, heaven forbid, your buddy will help you. Boy, girl, I don't care—but you need to stick to each other like superglue."

"Even in the bathroom?" a little kid asked, to hoots of laughter from his friends.

"Thank you for making the inevitable bathroom joke," Damon said. "Your buddy can wait outside—and check to make sure you've washed your hands. Now, one more thing: these vans will serve as your posse for the day. There's too many of us to travel en masse, so the counselors and campers you ride with are the people you will spend the day with. Make sure you end up with people you can stand. Clear on this? Great. Go find a buddy, and we'll load up the vans."

Olivia didn't need any encouragement. She raced across the lot to the Bass Cliff boys.

"Excited?" Adeline asked me. The purple straps of her swimsuit peeked out from under the straps of her dazzlingly white tank top. She wore a floppy, battered hat, the kind a fisherman might wear. One week and a major rainstorm in, and she looked just as put-together as she had when she arrived.

"Shauna thinks we're going to Sleeping Bear," I said. "What do you think?"

"I don't know," Adeline said, "but it doesn't really matter, does it?"

"No." I beamed back. "It absolutely doesn't."

Damon called, "Two spots left in Van One! Where's my final pair of buddies? Okay, Van One's full. Seat belts on, everyone. Van Two! Who's ready? I need twelve campers in Van Two, on the double."

Just then Olivia hurtled back into view, her ponytail frazzled, her face blotchy.

"Olivia! What's wrong?" I said.

"It's Noel." Tears welled in her eyes. "He changed his mind."

"What? Why would he do that?"

"I don't know." She gulped. "He said I was too clingy, that I never leave him alone! Why would he say that, Melly? He's the one who's been asking me to play all week. If he didn't want to be around me, he didn't have to ask."

"I don't know," I said, hugging her. "It doesn't make any sense to me either. He sucks."

Olivia stepped back and pressed the heels of her hands to her eyes. She took a deep breath. "It's okay. I can deal. I just don't get what I did wrong."

"You didn't do anything wrong. He's a jerk."

"I know." She took the elastic from her ponytail, shook out her hair, and pulled it back, higher than before. "I should've stuck with you from the beginning. At least he ditched me now, instead of halfway through the trip. We can still be buddies, right, Mel?"

"Oh," I said. "Actually. . ."

A shadow crossed Olivia's face. "Right. Of course. You found someone else." Then she brightened. "But it's not too late to switch."

"Olivia," I said, and stopped. Adeline was standing just a few feet away, waiting, watching, her face carefully blank. "I . . . don't think I can."

"What do you mean?" Olivia said. "Yeah, it's a little awkward, but I can do the talking if you're too scared. I'm sure they'll understand. I'm your best friend, and there are—what do you call them—extenuating circumstances."

"No," I said, reeling the word up from my gut like a stone from the bottom of a well. It was heavy. It was hard. And it came out louder than I meant. "I don't want to switch."

Olivia looked like she'd been slapped all over again. "Melly?" she said. Not like *Melly, what do you mean?* or *Melly, how could you say that to me?* but *Melly, is that really you?*

That was what decided it for me—that after the past week, my best friend no longer seemed to know me. Whether it was because she'd forgotten or because I'd changed I didn't know. But I wasn't the person she thought I was, not judging by the shock in her eyes.

I was used to feeling pulled along by Olivia. I liked it, even. She pulled me forward, to new and exciting places I wouldn't go on my own: attending Ms. Estrada's instrument petting zoo, starting a band, going to camp. But ever since we'd arrived at Camp Rockaway, she'd been pulling away from me, only connecting when it suited her.

And when we were together, it felt like she was pulling me backward, away from the things I wanted. Away from the lake, away from the raft, away from my new friends and especially Adeline. It wasn't fair for Olivia to pull me away from her, just because Noel had turned out to be a total butthead.

Adeline came over and laid a hand on my arm. "Melly, hey, there's room in Yasmina's van, but we have to go now."

Olivia's eyebrows went up, and I could hear her thinking, *Gladeline?* But I didn't care.

"We'll talk about this tonight," I promised, giving her one more quick hug. I might be frustrated, but I wasn't heartless. "Try to have fun without him, okay? You're awesome, and he's a jerk. You shouldn't let him ruin your day."

I hurried after Adeline and scrambled into the

waiting van. Damon slammed the sliding door after us. I didn't look back.

We bumped along the dirt road away from camp. Skip drove, Blair sat shotgun, and Armani passed out breakfast from a cooler. Granola bars, fruit, juice boxes, hardboiled eggs, cheese sticks, and best of all: Pop-Tarts. There was barely any radio reception near Camp Rockaway, but we sang along to static-filled oldies and country songs, belting so loud my ears rang and Blair threatened to put on talk radio.

The ride grew long—not as long as the ride back to Kalamazoo would be, but close. I leaned my head against the window, my eyes drifting shut, until someone shouted, "Michigan's Adventure! We're going to Michigan's Adventure, aren't we?" Sure enough, we passed a billboard showing screaming, happy people on a roller coaster, on a water slide, eating cotton candy. It was only five miles away.

"Wow," Adeline said. "I guess they felt like they had to make up for last year."

"What happened?" I asked. Toni and Shauna hadn't mentioned any disasters. Maybe they'd blocked it out.

"The way I heard it, some parent complained that our camp dollars weren't going to a 'thematically appropriate activity,' so we went to the Music House Museum in Traverse City. It's a museum about the history of musical instruments and stuff. It was okay, but kind of like school. And even though we went on speedboat rides afterward, and got dinner at this marina drive-in, it was not the most popular field trip."

"There won't be anything remotely educational about today!" Yasmina said. "I can't wait to go on the Thunderhawk. I heard it's like flying, but really scary."

"What about you, Melly?" Adeline asked. "You have any favorite rides?"

Not the Thunderhawk. Then again, I'd survived a whole week of firsts. "I'm up for almost anything," I said.

"That's the spirit," she said, hugging me around the shoulders.

At the amusement park entrance, the counselors passed out our admission wristbands. I caught Olivia watching me from across the crowd. She shook her head slowly, sadly. I gave her an encouraging thumbs-up, and she turned away. I hoped once she'd been on a few rides she'd forget Noel. While she was at it, she could forget me. She'd been doing it all week, after all.

I felt guilty, but only a twinge. *Things always have to be about her. Can't just one day be about me?*

"Okay, Van Three," Blair said. "Skip and Armani and I have been talking, and we think it would be smart to start the day on the water park side and then come back over for the rides."

"But it'll be hotter in the afternoon," someone protested.

"Exactly," Blair said. "If we do the water park now, we won't have to compete with all the people waiting until it's super hot. Besides, do you really want to ride all the way back to camp in a soggy swimsuit?"

When she put it that way, almost everyone agreed. Armani passed around a bottle of sunscreen, and away we went.

All morning, we slid down water slides, rode inner tubes on the Lazy River, and swam in the wave pool. It seemed like every five minutes the counselors were making us run to the drinking fountains to rehydrate. By the time Blair announced it was time for lunch, I wasn't sure what I wanted to do more: take a nap or eat a moose. Instead we went to the concession area, where I ordered a slice of veggie pizza and some French fries, just like Adeline.

The afternoon went by slower, mainly because the lines were longer. But it was still fun. I went on every ride with Adeline, even on the Wolverine Wildcat, which was old and wooden and so rickety my teeth rattled; even on the Shivering Timbers, which was twice as tall and made me light-headed just looking at it. I was terrified every moment, but I was glad I'd done it.

Adeline surprised me by balking at the Flying Trapeze.

"You're kidding me," I said. "You just went on the Thunderhawk. That's way scarier."

She shrugged. "Not to me. On the Flying Trapeze, you're dangling in those little chairs, swinging out so far you're almost sideways. I always think the chains are going to break and send me spinning into the next county."

"I think it's cool. It reminds me of little spiders, spinning out on their lines of silk," I said.

"Don't work your poetic wiles on me," Adeline growled.

"What if I just ask?" I said. "I did go on the Thunderhawk with you. Which, honestly, scared the crap out of me."

"I could tell by the way you screamed bloody murder the entire time. My ears are still ringing!" she said.

"Fine. I'll give it a try. But if the chains break—"

"I'll make sure we play a very nice song at your funeral."

The Flying Trapeze was way bigger than the swings at the Kalamazoo County Fair, but that only made it more magical. From the moment the machine hoisted us into the air and we began to spin gently out, farther and farther, I was enchanted. I could see the tops of the trees—the other rides—the water park. I looked for

Lake Michigan but couldn't quite see it. I let go of the chains and held out my arms.

I was at the machine's mercy. Even if I hadn't been hurtling through the air, I couldn't escape my chair until the ride stopped and they unlocked the safety bars. I could've felt helpless. I could've felt trapped. But I didn't. I felt safe and powerful. I felt free.

Adeline sat with her hands firmly on the chains, a determined expression on her face. "Hey, look," I yelled. "No hands!" She shook her head at me and smiled, and my heart lifted its wings and flew higher still.

It was the most wonderful feeling.

"Okay," Blair said afterward, checking her watch, "we've got time for two more rides. What'll it be?"

"It's so hot," someone moaned. "Can we please go on some water rides?"

"It's up to you. Just don't blame me when you ride back to camp with a soggy butt."

We went on the Grand Rapids first. All of us, even Armani and Skip, fit on two round rafts. Water sloshed around us as we bumped through the obstacle course. Whenever we hit a rock or went down a slide, waves gushed over the side. And when we went under the waterfall at the end, everyone got drenched. Blair, who'd stayed on dry land to watch our stuff, smirked as we exited, dripping. But none of us cared.

The Flying Trapeze would've been the perfect way

to dry off, but almost everyone wanted to try something new. We lined up for the HydroBlaster instead.

"It sounds like something a plumber would use to unclog a toilet," Adeline said.

"Close," Skip said. "It's a kind of pressure washer. You use it to hose off scum that's stuck on really bad. I once used one on a boat I was restoring."

"Sounds like heaps of fun. Maybe I'll sit this one out, too," said Blair.

"Relax," Yasmina said. "It's another raft ride. The catch is it's completely in the dark."

"All right," Blair said. "Just remember, it's the last one. So make it count."

These rafts held only two people. Adeline and I were last to board our little sky blue raft. I sat in front, my knees squished to my chest. Behind me, Adeline's knees hugged my hips. We waited in the dark as the rafts ahead of us lurched forward, screams echoing up the dark tunnel toward us.

"Melly?" Adeline said in a low voice. "Can I ask you something?"

"Yeah?" I whispered back, twisting to face her.

"I was wondering—" she began.

Then the raft started to slide forward, fast, and I hurried to face forward.

But not before Adeline's lips touched mine.

twenty

We hurtled downward into the blackness, water splashing around us. The slide twisted this way and that, sending us swinging far to one side, then the other. But I barely noticed. My heart and stomach and brain were doing far more elaborate acrobatics. Had Adeline really kissed me? Or was it just a bump, an accident, as the raft suddenly started moving?

The ride couldn't have lasted longer than a verse of "Ring Around the Rosie," but by the time our raft burst out of the chute into the sunlight, I'd experienced a symphony's worth of emotions. I blinked and climbed out shakily, my knees unsteady. My fingers rose to my face. My lips buzzed.

Adeline bent to tie her shoe. When she stood, she flashed her usual grin. "Fun ride, huh?"

"Um, yeah," I said. Had I imagined it? Maybe it

hadn't been Adeline's lips I'd felt. Maybe it was her hand, or her hair.

No. Lips did not feel like fingers. They did not feel like hair. Accidentally or on purpose, Adeline had kissed me.

"Kind of a tame one to go out on, if you ask me," Yasmina said.

Adeline shrugged. "I guess it was a little tame. But I liked it."

A little tame, but she liked it? Was she serious?

"Looks like it knocked the wind out of Melly," Yasmina said.

"I'm okay," I said. "Just a little dizzy."

I was quiet on the ride back to camp. We all were, compared to the ride down, but I barely said a word. I felt like I'd swallowed a seed. It had sprouted in my stomach, and now it was sending out tendrils— creeping, curling, leafing, blooming. Growing dark, tiny berries that made my mouth tingle. Did everyone's first kiss make them feel this way? My fingertips drifted to my lips again, but I lowered them quickly in case Adeline noticed.

She sat so close to me our arms and knees brushed, so close we knocked into each other when the van took a turn. Every time we made contact, my heart beat faster. Was Adeline talking louder than normal? I couldn't tell. I felt like all my senses had been scraped raw—every touch, every scent, every sound was *more.*

For days I'd felt there was something special about Adeline. I'd known she liked me as a friend, and of course I'd liked her. I'd wandered camp hoping to find her and lit up like a giddy firefly when I did. But it had never occurred to me to kiss her.

Now that she'd kissed me, it seemed so obvious. Of course I wanted to kiss her. Of course that was what that shiver down my spine, that glow in my belly, meant. It wasn't so different from my crush on Arjit, except it was even stronger. It had only taken me so long to recognize it because I wasn't expecting it—not at Camp Rockaway, and not a girl.

It was funny that all this time my friends had been pushing me toward David. Even I'd begun to see his potential. But something was missing. It was like the time Dad forgot to put baking powder in Mom's birthday cake. The batter looked perfectly normal when he poured it in the pan, but it refused to rise in the oven. It came out a vanilla-flavored hockey puck.

Why Adeline and not David? I didn't know. Of course everybody couldn't like everybody. There'd be total chaos: Olivia, Candace, and Noel times a billion. Still, I wondered if meeting Adeline had flipped a switch inside me. Would I only like girls now, or was she an exception to the rule?

Or maybe there were no rules. Maybe you had to let your heart work on a case-by-case basis.

My bigger question was, how could Adeline leave me in the parking lot with a squeeze on the arm and a promise to see me later, no explanation, no indication of what she was thinking? She was acting like nothing had happened, when I knew nothing would be the same again.

Our counselors sent us up to the lodge. The kitchen staff had the day off, so dinner was simple: sub sandwiches, salad, and Popsicles on the lawn. Everyone looked sunburned. Everyone looked tired. Everyone looked happy—almost. I found Olivia sitting alone at the fringe. Her eyes flickered up at me for a second, then dropped away. She kept chewing, not saying a word.

I'm not sure why people talk about having to face the music when they're in trouble, because to me there's nothing worse than a stony silence. I'd seen this look on Olivia's face before: her dark eyes black in the shadow of her furrowed brow, her mouth pinched shut. The difference was that I'd never seen her look at me this way, with this mixture of anger and disappointment and hurt. I'd never given her a reason to.

I took a deep breath and decided to copy Adeline

and pretend everything was normal. Maybe pretending was all it would take to make it true. I settled on the grass beside her, balancing my plate on my lap. "Hey. How was your day?"

She surprised me by answering almost normally, too. "Okay."

I tried again. "I never thought we'd go somewhere as cool as Michigan's Adventure."

She shrugged. "It was all right."

"I heard it was one of the best trips yet," I said, feeling bolder. "Adeline said last year they went to a music history museum and—"

"Oh, Adeline said, did she?"

I could've kicked myself. Was I trying to rub my decision in Olivia's face?

"You know how you told me not to let Noel ruin my day?" Olivia said, her voice growing louder. "Guess what. He didn't. You did."

"Olivia, I—"

"Your best friend, who you've known almost your entire life, gets ditched by the boy she likes, in front of all his friends. And what do you do? You run off with some random."

Her words stung. Adeline was anything but *some random*—to me, at least. "I had to. If I'd ditched Adeline, I wouldn't have been any better than Noel."

"Really? Let's consider that a moment." Olivia's voice was tight and high. "First of all, I'm pretty sure Noel didn't ditch me because his best friend was in trouble. You were right, he's a jerk, plain and simple. He likes my bass chops more than he likes me. Second, it wasn't an either-or situation. You could've been Adeline's buddy without ditching me. All you had to do was wait for a van with room enough for all of us. But no. You hightailed it as soon as you got the chance. You didn't even look back to see who I ended up with."

There was absolutely nothing I could say to that. She was 100 percent right.

"Anyway, it didn't matter who I ended up with because all I could think about was how my best friend completely abandoned me on one of the worst days of my life. Can you imagine what that felt like, Melly? For Noel to say the things he said in front of all his friends, and me not able to say a word without sounding like everything he said was true? I needed you. I needed my best friend, and you completely failed me." Tears cascaded down her cheeks.

I felt like there was a bone lodged in my throat. I struggled to whisper around it. "I'm sorry. I'm really, really sorry."

And I was. Would it have killed me, this morning, to say, *Hey, Adeline, let's all wait for the next van so Olivia can come, too*? It probably would've been fine. It probably would've been fun. But I wasn't looking that far ahead. All I could think was how I didn't want to spend another ounce of energy on Olivia.

My moment of selfishness had ruined her entire day. I'd known she was hurting, and I'd gone anyway. I was a terrible person, a terrible friend.

"Olivia, it was a really bad thing I did. Please forgive me."

She didn't answer for a long moment. Then she whispered, "Do you know what he said to me, in front of everyone? He said, 'Bros before hos.' Why would he call me that, Melly? I've never even kissed a boy, except for Truth or Dare. There's no way he could know about that."

"It's just a saying," I said. "A mean one. You know that."

"I can't believe I have to play in a band with him all week," Olivia said. She began crying again, her plate shaking so hard in her hands it threatened to spill on her lap. "And Candace! She sure didn't waste any time. I heard Noel won a pink teddy bear in one of the carnival games and gave it to her."

I took both our plates and set them on the grass, even though ants would be all over them in seconds. "Come here." Olivia cried into my shirt as I rubbed her back, saying, "Shh, it's okay, it's going to be okay." And I was grateful, after what I'd done, that she let me.

All night I dreaded seeing Adeline again. No, that's not right. I wanted to see her, more than anything, but the Olivia situation complicated things. Every time Adeline tried to catch my eye, I did my best to pretend I hadn't noticed, even though my heart ricocheted against my ribs. Finally, after band practice on Monday, I couldn't avoid her any longer. As we were packing up our gear, she said, "Want to hang out after B-flat?"

"I can't," I said, feeling sick. "I told Olivia I'd hang out with her."

Adeline's brow crinkled. "Well, what if the three of us hung out together?"

I remembered the disgust in Olivia's voice as she'd called Adeline *some random*. I wanted to believe she didn't blame Adeline for what I'd done, but I had my doubts. She'd been so angry and hurt. "I'm sorry," I said. "I don't think that's the best idea."

"Okay . . . ," Adeline said.

"Because of yesterday," I began, planning to tell her what Noel did to Olivia, and how I hadn't wanted to deal with the aftermath. Spending today with Olivia, doing whatever she wanted, was the best way I could make it up to her. It had nothing to do with Adeline.

But Adeline's face was a door slamming shut. "It's fine. You don't have to explain."

"It's only because—"

"Seriously, Melly. It's okay. No big deal."

"Tomorrow, maybe," I said. "Or even tonight, at fire-bowl." I trailed off, imagining the look on Olivia's face if I said, *Hey, let's sit near Adeline,* imagining her saying, *That random? Why?* I knew it wouldn't happen.

"Sure," Adeline said, already half out the door. "Of course. I'll see you around."

I walked alone to the lodge for lunch.

What if I were to tell Olivia, *Look, I know I've only known Adeline for a week*—eight days, I couldn't help correcting myself—*but she's not just some random. She's different.*

Would Olivia understand? Would Olivia hear anything besides, *You've found someone you like better than me*?

What if I were to tell Olivia, *She kissed me, and I liked it*?

It didn't help that at practice Adeline had treated me exactly the same as before the kiss. Was that normal? People kissed, out of the blue, and life went on, ob-la-di, ob-la-da?

It used to be Olivia and I always told each other everything. The thing was, until now there hadn't been much for me to tell. More had happened in the last two weeks than in the whole rest of my life, it felt like, first with my parents and now this.

Yet I didn't want to talk about either. My parents, because I didn't want to think about them. Adeline, because I did. I cupped my memory of what happened on the HydroBlaster like a tiny flame in my hands. As long as I sheltered it, I could enjoy its glow. It would grow. But if I held it in the open, the wind might puff it out.

Now Adeline was upset, too. I could hardly blame her.

"How are you doing?" I asked Olivia over our macaroni and cheese. She had a pinched look about her. Her eyes looked bruised. "How was practice?"

She sighed heavily. "I'm here, aren't I? It didn't kill me."

"For which Damon is grateful, I'm sure," I said. "He wouldn't want your parents to sue." I held my breath, hoping Olivia would catch the joke. Maybe even toss it back.

"My parents don't have the money to sue," she said. "They spent it all sending me here. More's the pity."

She gave a small smile, and I knew things were okay—between us, anyway. That was the most important thing. It was Olivia I'd be returning to Kalamazoo with at the end of the week. I might never see anyone else from Camp Rockaway again, especially not Adeline, who lived at the opposite end of the state.

The thought of never seeing Adeline again made the macaroni in my stomach turn to cement. Even though we hadn't touched since the van ride back to camp, I still felt a string tying our wrists together. Every time she moved, I felt it. Right now she was sitting at a table in the far opposite corner of the lodge. Now she was hopping up from the table to get a refill on applesauce from the kitchen window. Now it was B-flat, and she was completely out of sight, but I could still feel her, lying on her cot a couple of tents away, though I didn't know what she was doing. Writing in her notebook, probably.

To my surprise, Poppy delivered two letters for me. One was from Grandma Schiff. From the page I could practically hear her concerned clucking: I must be reeling from the news as much as she was, and I should do my best to have a good time at camp and leave the grown-up matters to the grown-ups, and why didn't I visit her and Grandpa in Valparaiso for a few days before school started up again? I thought the other might finally be from Dad, but no.

Dear Melly,

It's Thursday, and I'm running out of ways to entertain myself. Laundry done, bathroom scrubbed, house vacuumed, bills paid. I've been listening to Danielle Steel audiobooks the entire time. Don't judge.

Speaking of the bathroom, I was noticing how tired it's looking. Funny how you can see the same thing every day of your life, and it all looks perfectly fine. Then one day, poof: you think, who the heck chose this wallpaper? I stopped at the Home Depot for paint chips. How does Perfectly Peach sound to you?

I bet you're having so much fun the time is flying by for you. I'm thinking of you often.

Lots of love,

Mom

PS: There's still time to write to your mother!

I rolled my eyes. Hello, Mom! Could you be any more obvious? If I were writing an essay for English class about this letter, the first thing I'd have said was, *The bathroom is a metaphor for my parents' pathetic marriage; my father is the dingy, out-of-date wallpaper.* Or was that my mother? Anyway, it was clear she didn't actually want my opinion on redecoration. She'd already made up her mind. What did she expect me to write back? *Dear Mom, Perfectly Peach sounds perfectly peachy! How about new tile and fixtures while you're at it?*

One thing was sure: Mom had picked the right room for her metaphor. Life was in the toilet. I crumpled up the letter and shoved it into my suitcase with the first.

"We're still on for this afternoon, right?" Olivia said.

"Mm-hm," I said. "Once staring practice is over."

"Once *what* is over?"

Oh, right. Olivia had been so out of touch with my life, she had no idea what I was talking about. I said, "David and I are supposed to practice our nonverbal communication skills."

"Oh," Olivia said. "Sounds intriguing." She waggled her eyebrows.

"It's not like that. It's kind of weird, but I actually think it's helping. I used to think David was stuck-up, but now I think he's just shy. This helps him be not so scared of me."

"There's a name for that," Shauna said. "Exposure therapy."

"What's that?" Olivia asked.

"When people have phobias of spiders or snakes or whatever, they stick 'em in a room with those things until they stop being afraid. Perfectly safe, of course."

"So you're saying David has Melliphobia," said Olivia. "Awesome."

"I want a phobia named after me!" Toni said.

I rolled my eyes. "Thanks. Thank you for comparing me to spiders and snakes."

"Some of my best friends are spiders and snakes,"

Olivia said, and we all laughed.

This, I thought, pushing away the memory of Adeline's lips on mine. *This is what really matters. More than crushes. More than anything.*

twenty-one

The past week might as well have not happened. Adeline didn't speak to me anymore except about music. There was no diving, no canoeing, no talking about our lives outside of camp. I spent Monday afternoon pounding away in a practice stall with Olivia until the air grew foggy with our sweat, until the ache in my arms pulled my mind from the ache in my chest. The lake was a distant blue dream.

By the end of practice Tuesday morning, I couldn't stand it anymore. I ran after Adeline on the way to lunch. My palms were practically gushing water. "Adeline!"

She barely glanced at me, continuing up the path. "Yeah?"

I pulled up beside her, panting. "I feel like you think I'm mad at you or something. But I'm not. It's Olivia."

"Olivia's mad?"

Already I was explaining it wrong. "Sort of. I mean, she's jealous. Of you and me."

"Did you tell her?" Adeline asked.

"Tell her what?"

"About what happened. On the HydroBlaster."

It was the first time she'd acknowledged anything had happened. I still couldn't tell how she felt about it. Whether it had been a mistake. "No, I didn't," I said. "It was . . . private."

"Ah," Adeline said.

From that single syllable, I could tell I'd said absolutely the wrong thing.

"Did you *want* me to tell everyone?" I said, a little annoyed.

"I didn't say anything about telling everyone." Her voice was like a guitar string, getting wound up higher and tenser. "Who said anything about telling everyone?"

"I don't know what to do," I said. "I don't know what you want from me, but Olivia's been my friend forever, and she's the one I'm going home with when camp is over. And with everything happening in my family right now, I'm going to need her. If I have to choose between making you happy and making her happy, the choice is pretty obvious."

Adeline looked at me strangely, and I was sure she

was going to lose her cool. I almost wished she would. Then I'd feel better about avoiding her.

She said, "Maybe the real problem is you think that's what you're choosing between."

I stopped walking. My face grew hot. "What's that supposed to mean?"

"Making Olivia happy. Making me happy. Why is that even the question?" Adeline shook her head. "Never mind. I can see you have no idea what I'm talking about."

She walked ahead, leaving me staring after her. She was right. I didn't know what she was talking about. Why didn't she just tell me what she thought I should do? I hadn't fixed a thing. Maybe I'd even made things worse.

Then, at B-flat, came the letter I'd been waiting for.

Melly Girl

Sorry it's taken me so long to write. It's not because I haven't been thinking about you. It's because I've been trying to think of the right words.

I know Mom doesn't want to get into the whys and wherefores, but I think we owe you an explanation. I only apologize that I'm not telling you in person, but the truth is I'm a big chicken. Insert eggs-cruciating joke here.

Here it is, Mouse. Falling in love is a wonderful feeling,

maybe the best feeling in the world. Some people say it makes you do stupid things, but I never saw it that way. Your mom and I met twenty years ago, and I haven't regretted a moment of it. She's a wonderful person, and I couldn't ask for a better daughter.

But twenty years is a long time. Some couples, if they're lucky, grow together. Some grow apart. I don't know why we ended up in the second group. Maybe it's because we were so young when we got married. We barely knew a life outside of our parents, and suddenly we were building a life together. We never got a chance to find out who we were on our own. That's one theory, anyway.

I know you don't have firsthand romantic experience (and if I'm wrong, we need to have a serious dad-daughter talk when you get home!) so I'll just tell you: falling in love can happen in an instant, but falling out of love can take years. I'm guessing our news hit you like a bombshell last weekend. But it didn't come out of nowhere, not for your mom and me. There were problems. Some we tried to ignore. Others we tried to work through. But in the end, we agreed we're better off as friends. That's one thing that's never changed between us.

That's enough heavy stuff for one letter. I hope you're having a good time at camp. I love you, and I can't wait to see you play.

Big hugs,
Dad

I went still and cold, the blood draining from my face, my fingers icy. My grip on the paper slackened. It sagged in my lap. If you'd asked me how I felt in that moment, I couldn't have answered. I didn't feel sad, exactly. I didn't even feel angry. I was empty. I was nothing.

All this time, I'd been sure Olivia was right: there was some big reason my parents were splitting up. Not something fixable, necessarily, but something logical. But Dad's explanation wasn't any more satisfying than Mom's lack of one. Falling out of love didn't sound like a reason at all. It sounded like an excuse—something you told your kid so you wouldn't have to tell the truth.

And if he *was* telling the truth, that was even worse. Because if falling out of love was as random as he made it sound, why would anyone bother falling *in* love to begin with?

Except probably you couldn't help it. It just happened. And then twenty years might pass before you realized you'd made a terrible mistake. In the meantime, you had a kid, and in getting your life back, you had to screw up theirs. Hypothetically speaking.

"Hey," Olivia whispered. "Is that a letter from your dad?"

I nodded. My eyes weren't watering. My chin wasn't crumpling. But I was afraid that might change if I opened my mouth. I wadded up the letter and put it with the others.

"Are you okay?"

I shrugged and lay back against my pillow. Eventually I'd have to tell her what the letter said, give her the big reveal, but I couldn't do it now, not with Shauna and Toni a few feet away.

When B-flat was over, Olivia walked quietly with me up to the lodge. She went to get her bass. I went to find David. At least staring practice meant I didn't have to talk—not that David was much of a conversationalist.

He was waiting outside for me. Without speaking, he led me into the stall he'd signed out. He shut the door, and we sat cross-legged facing each other. It had become routine.

But as I started the timer on my watch, I couldn't focus—not just my mind, but my eyes. There, suddenly, were the tears that had refused to fall. They'd been there all along, dammed up. But something had knocked a chink in the dam. First came a trickle. Then came a flood.

David jumped backward in alarm. I drew up my knees and pressed my face against them, gulping in air, trying to calm myself. But I was too far gone. Something about this quiet room, this quiet boy, had given me permission to let go. I'd thought I felt nothing, but my emotions had been lying in wait. Now they stampeded.

"Melly!" David hissed. "Melly, what's wrong?"

I shook my head and tried to wipe my eyes with the back of my hand, but there were too many tears for it to do any good. David untied his bandanna, the one I'd made him, and passed it to me. I clutched it, pressing the soft cotton against my eyes. It was quickly drenched, but it did the job. I stopped crying.

"I'm so sorry," I mumbled. "I'll wash your bandanna."

"Don't worry about that," David said. "Just, are you okay?"

"Yeah." *Why am I even pretending? He saw me completely lose it.* "My parents are getting divorced. I guess it's getting to me."

"Oh," he said. "Oh."

"I know. People get divorced every day of the year. I'm being ridiculous."

"No, I get it. My parents split up a few years ago."

"I bet you didn't break down in front of random people."

"Are you kidding? I cried for a week. Even at school."

"Still," I said, "you were just a little kid."

"I was nine," David said. "Not that little."

He picked at his shoelaces. I wiped my sore eyes.

"What was it like?" I asked. "At your house, I mean."

"It was weird. We were all still living together at first, but it was like a bizarro version of home. Have you ever seen *Invasion of the Body Snatchers*?"

I shook my head.

"It's this really old sci-fi movie. These aliens take over people's brains. They look the same as always, but they're not themselves anymore. Suddenly my dad, he switched to second shift and started sleeping in the den. And my mom, she told me it was time I learned to cook. My sister got more chores, too. It was so random. But they acted like it was totally normal—all cheerful to our faces."

"Did they fight a lot with each other? Before they decided to break up?"

"Oh, yeah. Before, during, after. But only in their bedroom. They'd go in there and scream their heads off. We'd have to turn the volume on the TV all the way up. But when they were done they'd come out and pretend nothing had happened. I'm telling you, body snatchers."

"What'd they fight about?" I asked.

"Everything." David shrugged. "Money, a lot of the time. My dad likes to spend it, my mom doesn't. She was always saying, 'How are you going to send three kids to college if you keep buying that crap?' He barely even pays child support. Those extra chores she gave us? She was thinking ahead. She had to get a second job."

"But you're here," I said, not sure how to finish the thought without sounding rude.

"On scholarship," David said. "She just had to get me here. She tries, you know?"

We were quiet a moment.

I said, "Were you mad at them?"

"Are you kidding?" said David. "I was furious—at my dad, mostly. I mean, he's not a bad person. He loves me and all. But he's not what you'd call responsible, and I can't blame my mom for not putting up with him. She gave him so many second chances. I guess you can't even call them second chances. There were like five hundred of them."

"Did it take a long time?" I asked. "To stop being mad?"

"Yeah." David sighed. "Yeah, it did. I stopped crying way before I stopped being mad."

Neither of us said anything for a long moment. Finally I said, "Thanks. You're the first person I've really talked to about this. And thanks for not freaking out when . . . when *I* did."

"I was a little freaked out," David said, and we laughed.

"Let's do our staring practice," I said. "Olivia's probably wondering where I am."

We got back into position, and I reset my watch. Staring at each other was still weird, but I had to give

Donna credit. Not only had our playing improved, but I also felt like I understood David better as a person. How could I have ever thought him rude? His wide brown eyes, when I could see them, were soft and kind.

Suddenly I realized those wide brown eyes weren't open anymore. David's face came closer as he leaned toward me. I pushed myself backward, yelping, "What are you doing?"

His eyes flew open, and he shot back across the room. "Nothing!"

"You were going to—" I couldn't even finish the sentence.

"I thought you wanted to," he protested.

"What possibly made you think that?"

"The way you looked at me."

"Only because Donna told us to!"

"And we were talking."

"Because I was upset. And you actually seemed to know how I was feeling."

"And you gave me this bandanna."

"Because your stupid hair was in your stupid face all the time!"

Hurt swept over him. "I'm sorry," I said. "I don't really think your face is stupid. But, God!" I jumped to my feet, barely remembering to grab my stick bag, and ran out of the stall.

Why had David spoiled a perfectly good moment

trying to kiss me? It had felt so good to let go of all that junk that had built up inside me. What if he'd only been nice because he was trying to butter me up? The thought sickened me. I'd trusted him, but I'd been wrong before. I was wrong all the freaking time.

I forgot to meet Olivia. Or maybe I didn't forget, exactly. All I knew was I had to get away, fast, before David decided to come after me. If I hadn't permanently scared him away—which honestly I wouldn't have minded. I ran from the lodge, not knowing where I was going, where I'd end up. But when I got there, it made perfect sense: the infirmary.

The infirmary was attached to the back of the camp office, another cabin in the woods. The nurse looked up, startled, as I threw open the door with a bang. "Are you okay?" she asked.

I nodded. I was breathing hard, and my face felt swollen. "I just need to lie down."

"You do that," she said. "But first, I'd like to take your temperature. You're flushed. And would you like to wash your face?"

I splashed cold water on my face in the bathroom. Afterward I took a cot by the window, facing into the deep trees. The nurse poked a thermometer under my tongue.

"Ninety-nine point one," she said. "A little high, but probably nothing to worry about. Here. Have some water. You lie down, cool off, and relax for as long as you need to, okay?"

I took a sip. "I forgot to flip my pick."

"That's okay, we know you're here. What's your name, hon?"

"Melly Goodwin."

"Okay, Melly. If there's any change in how you feel, better or worse, I'll be right in the other room. Just give a holler."

The springs dug through the flimsy, Pine-Sol–scented mattress and squeaked irritably as I squirmed to get comfortable. I couldn't. What a day. What a week. My parents, Dad especially, dumping the divorce on me. Olivia keeping me from Adeline. David—the one person I'd thought out-shrank me in the shrinking violet department—trying to kiss me. None of these things was my fault, but why did everyone act like I'd stand there and take whatever they threw at me?

Why couldn't I be more like my drums? Drums are strong. You can play them with all your might, yet they're almost impossible to break. They absorb each blow, but they don't take it quietly. The harder you hit them, the louder they yell.

Everyone thought because I was quiet I must not

care, I must not mind. They could speak for me, act for me, make decisions I'd be happy to go along with, because I wasn't fighting, was I? They didn't understand my quiet.

My quiet wasn't like dew gathering on the grass each morning, then evaporating in the sun. It wasn't like the moon watching silently from hundreds of thousands of miles away. My quiet was like a needle held in a flame, changing slowly from silver to red hot, to blinding orange, with a spark of blue at the point. I couldn't be quiet for much longer.

Four days to fix things with Adeline. Four days to figure out what, exactly, I was going to do when my parents showed up. They wanted to discuss the future calmly and rationally? All I wanted to do was scream at them for screwing up our lives. And how could they expect me to be rational when they were the ones making crazy decisions? They were the biggest hypocrites on the planet. Somehow I had to let them know it.

I rolled over and stared out the window into the greenery, willing answers to come to me. None did. Before long my eyes drifted closed.

I woke when the nurse poked her head back into the room and said softly, "Dinner's in a few minutes. Are you up for eating?" I sat up and realized I was hungry. I nodded and pulled myself out of bed to use the bathroom.

"One more temp check," she said afterward, handing back the thermometer. When I was finished, she read off the numbers. "Ninety-eight point six. You are perfectly normal."

"That's up for debate," I muttered.

She laughed. "That proves it. The girl who came in here a few hours ago never would've made a joke like that."

A few hours? Yikes. Olivia would be furious. I'd missed percussion workshop, too. I walked to the Fretboard. My pick still showed me as being at the lodge, so I left it alone. A line had begun outside. Olivia was sitting on the lawn, frowning. My stomach dropped, but I kept walking toward her.

"Where did you disappear to?" she demanded, jumping to her feet. "Don't tell me you were with *her.*"

Anger rose like bile in my throat. *Some random. Her.* If I'd been with a boy I liked, David or anyone else, Olivia would never talk about him that way. What did she have against Adeline?

"I got sick. I had to go to the infirmary," I told her.

"Without even telling me where you were going?" Olivia said. "I waited for you, you know. I searched for you. I even found David. He said he didn't know where you'd gone either. That you ran out of the room all of a sudden."

"I got sick." When she stared skeptically, I blurted,

"He tried to kiss me."

"He tried to—"

"Shhh!"

"He tried to kiss you?" Olivia repeated in a whisper. "Oh my God, Melly! How . . . ?"

"We were doing our staring practice. He closed his eyes and leaned in. It was weird."

"What were you thinking, running away? You could've had your first kiss!"

"I don't like him like that," I said, thinking, *Second kiss. Sort of.*

"You don't? But you said—"

"No, I didn't. You assumed."

"Still, you got sick? Was his breath, like, really bad or something?"

"No! It was . . ." Ugh! Why wasn't it enough that I hadn't wanted David to kiss me? To explain, I'd have to go into everything. The conversation he and I'd had. The letter—the awful letter—from my father. In the end I could only shrug.

"Well," Olivia said, more gently, "are you feeling better now?"

"Mostly," I said. What was one more little lie?

twenty-two

When Damon announced the winners of the second open mic drawing the next morning, Adeline's name was among them. Maybe it was stupid to wish she'd ask me to play with her, but I did, harder than anything. It would solve so much. I'd have to say yes—out of politeness, of course—and Olivia would have no right to get mad. I'd prove to Olivia that I could be friends with both of them. I'd prove to Adeline that everything since the field trip had been one big misunderstanding.

But when I sneaked a look at her, she was thick in conversation with Yasmina.

Toni said, "Hey, Mel. I'm debuting a new song tonight, and I want you on drums."

I glanced back at Adeline. She still wasn't looking at me. "Okay," I told Toni. "I'm in."

"Fabulous," said Toni. "We're practicing after B-flat."

I started to say something about staring practice, but I stopped. As far as I was concerned, that ritual was over.

At band practice, Donna noticed something was up. "People! What is going on with you?" she said, stopping us halfway through a song. "David and Melly, are you even listening to each other? Never mind *looking* at each other. What happened to all the progress you made?"

David ducked his head, his hair falling in his eyes. The bandanna was nowhere to be seen.

"Sorry," I said in a small voice.

"Don't be sorry!" Donna said. "Do better! We've only got three days until the show."

I counted us off once more. As we played, Adeline's eyes flickered curiously at David and me. But that was all: just a flicker. She'd given up on me. My throat swelled up. I had to do something before I went back to all that crap with Mom and Dad and never saw her again. I had to turn the next three days into something good. Otherwise—otherwise—

I didn't know how to finish the thought.

Just when I couldn't feel any worse, at the end of practice, Donna said, "Melly, please stick around. I'd like to talk to you."

I wasn't sure whether I should zip up my sticks or

not, whether I should stay behind the drums or stand up, so as the others packed up their instruments and left Trolltunga, I perched at the very edge of my stool, ready to snap to Donna's commands. I watched forlornly as the patch of woods beyond the doorway disappeared as she nudged the door closed with her foot. What did she want from me? When you were doing a good job, Donna ignored you. This was the opposite.

She surprised me by sitting cross-legged on the floor in front of the blackboard. She slapped the rug in front of her and said, "Come join me."

I almost tripped getting there as fast as I could. Donna looked at me with curiosity—and disappointment, too. "Really, Melly? Are you still scared of me?"

"I—" I didn't know what to say. *Yes, actually, terrified. Never underestimate my cowardice!* I shook my head no, wishing it weren't so obvious a lie.

"Lots of kids are scared at their auditions, and I get that I'm not the warmest, fuzziest person. But I thought in the past week we'd come to . . . an understanding." Donna shook her head. "Anyway. That's sort of related to what I wanted to talk about. Melly, is something going on I can help you with?"

My breath caught in my throat. She had to be talking about the David incident, but how did she know what had happened?

She said, "Last week, I heard you becoming more

and more confident as the days went by. A little stiff, yes, a little timid, but way more relaxed than the first time I heard you. But ever since we started up again Monday, it seems like you've had some kind of setback. I see you literally curling in on yourself. And today? Well, you and David already got an earful from me."

"I'm sorry," I whispered again.

Donna breathed out hard through her nose. "Melly. You don't owe me anything. But I don't want you to leave camp feeling disappointed in yourself. I get this sense that you're holding back. Tell me, how do you feel when you play at home?"

"Good, I guess. It's fun."

"So what's different here? Is it playing with other people that's giving you a hard time?"

"No," I said. "I mean, it's not easy playing with new people, but I'm getting used to it."

"That's encouraging," Donna said, but she didn't sound happy, only confused. She tapped her fingers on her chin. "Tell me. What do you think will happen if you let go?"

"Let go?" I remembered my tantrum last week. "I broke a stick the other day."

Donna smirked. "All right. I wasn't thinking in terms of property damage."

"I guess I don't know what you mean," I said. We were sitting as close as David and I had during staring practice, and I wished I could back up. But even as I turned my face away, I could feel Donna's eyes drawing mine back.

"Music isn't just playing notes on a page. You've got to put your heart into it," she said. "I'm not saying lose control. I'm saying let what's happening inside you come out."

"But what if you can't do one without the other?" I asked.

Donna waited a long moment. Then she said, "Ah."

"I love the drums," I said around the lump in my throat. "Usually they make me feel . . . I don't know. Brave, kind of. Strong. But some *things* have been happening lately."

"Things out of your control," Donna said. I nodded. "And you don't want that to happen on drums, too."

I stared at my hands. "Something like that. Maybe."

"Okay," Donna said. She frowned at the ceiling, as if the perfect thing to say was written up there. Too bad there was no perfect thing to say. I was hopeless.

I didn't expect her to say, "Remember Rebel Girl?"

Of course I remembered Rebel Girl. I remembered how she strutted around town, the object of admiration and envy and scorn, breaking every rule, each word people said about her rolling off her back. I remembered how different we were.

"You realize I picked that song for you," Donna said.

My mouth dropped open. "You did?"

"Don't act so surprised."

"I thought my song was 'Landslide,'" I said.

"'Landslide'? It doesn't even have a drum part," Donna said quizzically. "Oh, right—you mean because of the *things* in your life. I get it. But no. As soon as I met you, I thought, *This is a girl who needs to meet her inner rebel.*"

"What makes you think I have one?" I asked.

"Every girl has an inner rebel," said Donna. "But come on. You're a rocker. You're a drummer. You've got *rebel* written all over you, even if you haven't realized it yet."

I shook my head. It was a bunch of baloney. Yet this was Donna, with the stare that could see right through you. She didn't waste time on anything less than the truth.

"I want you to remember Rebel Girl when you play," Donna said. "I want you to *be* Rebel Girl. I'm not saying play loud and fast when the song isn't loud and fast. I'm not saying break sticks or, God forbid, crack cymbals. I'm saying let go of what other people think. I'm saying stop judging yourself so harshly—because I've got your number, Melly; I know you have been."

I nodded.

"Let me hear you say it," said Donna. "'I will be Rebel Girl.'"

"I will be Rebel Girl," I mumbled. This was way too cheesy, even for Camp Rockaway.

"I didn't catch that. What did you say?"

God, she was annoying. "I will be Rebel Girl!" I yelled.

Donna grinned her shark grin. "Good. Go get some lunch. I heard it's chicken nuggets."

As I ran to the lodge—though I don't know why I bothered; those chicken nuggets were going to be stone cold, anyway—I realized something crazy. I wasn't scared of Donna anymore.

That afternoon, Toni signed out a group practice stall with both drums and keyboard. But I stopped at the door when I saw who else had shown up for our rehearsal: Candace.

She was still hanging out with Noel, which meant Olivia still had a problem with her. I should have a problem with her, too. That was how it worked. The enemy of your friend was your enemy. Simple math. The associative property of friendship.

Except as far as I knew, liking the same jerky boy wasn't a crime. I walked in and said hi.

"Hey, Melly," Candace said, glancing up from her violin as she tuned. "I've been wanting to play with you for a while."

"You have?" I was stunned.

"Sure. Adeline's had nothing but good to say about you."

"She has?"

"Yeah. We're in the same tent, remember? We're always talking band stuff."

"Okay, ladies," Toni said. "I spent all of B-flat making this chart, even though I was supposed to write a letter to my cousins, so let's get down to business."

Hanging out with Toni was always fun, but I saw a whole new side of her as she slipped behind the keyboard. Her skinny fingers were strong, striding confidently over the keys. She set up a simple yet haunting hook with her right hand. A few measures in, she added her left, playing in counterpoint.

The two lines of melody were like two people on a dance floor, doing their own moves while keeping the same beat. They slid close one moment and spun apart the next, never quite colliding. Sometimes one hand echoed the other, but it almost seemed like an accident, because then they were off doing their own thing again.

As if that weren't impressive enough, Toni started rapping.

Folks underestimate me 'cause I'm flyweight
Like being petite means that somehow I don't rate
That sentiment makes me extremely irate

'Cause hell yeah I'm fly, but I ain't no lightweight
I'm here to create, won't be sedate, can you relate
Gonna strike a match, light my fuse, and activate

Watch out people, Ima blow your mind
I may be small, but I'm dynamite
Cover your head and take a step back 'cause
TNT comes in a cute little package

She sang that last part. Of course I already knew she had a great voice, but I had only heard her at firebowl. She must have worked hard to blend in then, because now as she let loose, her voice filled the small room and then some. It was rich and throaty and absolutely did not sound like it should be coming from a tiny thirteen-year-old girl. But then, that was the whole point of her song, wasn't it? Chalk me up as one more person who'd underestimated Toni.

She stopped abruptly after the first chorus and said, "Well?"

"Wow." The word slipped from my mouth.

"*Wow* is right," Candace said.

Toni's face split into a grin. "So, you two think you can work with that?"

"How do you do that?" I said. "I know a thing or two about limb independence, but for me, it's just rhythm.

— 245 —

You were playing one tune with your right hand, and playing a different one with your left hand, and singing a third."

Toni shrugged. "Guess I'm just awesome. You should hear me when I've got my looper pedal with me. I'm a freaking one-girl band."

"And so modest," Candace teased.

"I've never hidden my light under a bushel, and I'm not about to start now," said Toni. "Come on, ladies. Let's get to it. I've got a date with the beach after this."

We got to it. I couldn't remember ever playing drums to a rap song before. Not for the first time since coming to camp, I realized there were more gaps in Olivia's playlists than I'd ever stopped to think about. There was a whole galaxy of music out there, expanding every second, and I knew just a few little stars.

Candace played tentatively at first, bowing long notes in the background. But as Toni's lyrics grew bolder, Candace did as well, layering on a whole new voice with her violin.

I kept things simple. I didn't want to distract one bit from Toni. My drums were simply the beat her hands were dancing to. At the same time, I tried to hold on to what Donna had said. *Relax. You don't have to be perfect. Toni asked you to be her drummer for a reason. Stop judging yourself, and own it.* And I discovered the more energy I put into the drums, the more they fueled Toni's performance.

By the end, the song was downright intense. It was catchy, too. I'd be earwormed for the rest of the day.

"I knew I made the right choice with you two," Toni said. "Try it again from the top?"

Breathlessly we nodded. We played hard for another half hour.

Afterward I told Candace, "I've never seen anyone groove like that on violin before."

She grinned. "Thanks. My parents made me start learning classical when I was three, and I'm in the kids' symphony orchestra back home. But my soul belongs to rock 'n' roll."

I swung my stick bag over my shoulder. I was halfway out the door when Candace said, "Melly? Is Olivia mad at me?"

I turned and stared. "Um, yeah. I'm pretty sure."

"Do you know why?"

"Well . . . because . . . Noel."

Candace frowned. "But she knows I had nothing to do with what happened, right?"

"Didn't you? Last week, Noel liked Olivia, or it sure seemed that way. Now he likes you."

"I didn't steal him, Melly," she said. "I swear. He decided he didn't like her anymore all on his own. If she's going to get mad at someone, she should get mad at him, not me."

"She's mad at him, too," I said. "But what you did, jumping into her spot? Can you blame her for being upset?"

"What was I supposed to do?" Candace said helplessly. "I've liked him for years. Now that he's noticed me, I'm supposed to tell him no, just so I don't hurt Olivia's feelings?"

"I don't know," I said. "Maybe."

The truth was I wasn't sure. Why should Candace sacrifice her happiness for Olivia's? Noel was the one who'd broken Olivia's heart. Maybe it didn't matter what Candace did. Maybe it didn't matter what anyone did, as long as they made themselves happy. Maybe.

"Still," Candace said, "do you think you could talk to her? Things at band practice have been super awkward the past few days, and we need to focus on our performance on Saturday."

My mouth moved to say yes. The word almost escaped my lips. I stopped just in time. Olivia's drama was half the reason I now had my own. Did I really want to get sucked in?

"I think you and Olivia need to work this one out on your own," I said. And I left.

twenty-three

That night, it was my turn to freak out about what to wear to the open mic. All my clothes were wrinkled and damp and smelled like mushrooms.

"You can't wear that," Olivia said to my first choice, a T-shirt with different flavors of donuts printed on it. Mom had bought it for me, thinking it was cute. I thought so, too, until I tried it on and realized two of the donuts were located in the two worst possible places for donuts to be.

I made a face. "It's the only clean thing I have left, besides underwear."

"Well, you can't just wear underwear!"

"Believe it or not, I'm aware of that," I said.

Olivia picked through my suitcase. She pulled out a wad of paper. "What's this?"

"Nothing!" I peeled it from her grasp.

"Is that one of the letters from your parents? Why is it all crumpled up?"

"It's just garbage," I said, throwing it back into the suitcase. "Who cares? Now are you going to help me find something to wear or not?"

Olivia gave me a weird look. "Okay, chill. Wear this." She handed me a tank top with a butterfly on it.

"I wore that last week."

"Yeah, but there's no stains on it, and it doesn't have armpits, so it can't smell that bad."

I sniffed it. It had the same damp suitcase smell everything had, but that was it.

"And I've got to do your makeup," Toni told me.

"Me next, please," Shauna said, twirling across the tent. She'd been chosen, too. She wore full cow woman regalia, including a hat she'd gotten who knew where.

Finally we were ready to leave.

At the lodge, the four of us grabbed seats together near the stage. It was so different from last week, when Olivia ditched me for Noel. When Adeline nabbed me and I felt something change. My stomach twisted, and it wasn't just nerves. It was regret.

The pressure of opening fell to Shauna and her posse of Bass Cliff boys, who performed one of her feisty country anthems. It was hilarious in all the right ways. Everyone laughed and cheered. It was the reminder I needed that Camp Rockaway was the friendliest crowd ever.

Toni, Candace, and I were only third in the lineup, thankfully. I didn't have to spend too much time biting my nails. I hadn't been on a stage since our school's spring concert. Sitting behind the drums, squinting into the darkened room, dozens of people staring up at us from the audience, I remembered all at once how powerful and terrified all of this made me feel.

Relax. Let go. These are your friends, and they want to see you rock. It helped that Toni didn't betray a single raw nerve. I couldn't stay very anxious with her in the lead.

The true sign we'd won over our audience was when they started to clap along. Suddenly I wasn't alone on percussion. I was one drummer among dozens—but I was the leader. I held down the beat, and the audience followed. As for Toni, she was dynamite, all right, exploding with energy as her voice bounced off the walls of the lodge.

My friends hugged me as we came down from the stage and took our seats. My hands shook as I drank the lemonade waiting for me, but gradually I settled back in my chair—that is, until Damon said, "Now we have Adeline, performing an original song she calls 'Headlights.' Please welcome her to the stage!"

Adeline walked onstage alone. Her outfit wasn't fancy. She wasn't wearing makeup. The lights picked up every scar on the surface of her guitar. And somehow she was the most beautiful person I'd ever seen. Realizing that hurt.

She swung her guitar strap over her shoulder and adjusted the microphones, one for guitar, one for vocals. She looked solemnly into the darkness in the back of the lodge for a moment. Then she smiled and leaned into the mic. "Thanks," she said. She began to strum. She began to sing.

Gray skies, seems the rain will never end
Lonely, I could really use a friend
I thought you were just like me
Now I don't know, gotta wait and see

Wish I could be wherever you are
Whether it's Michigan, whether it's Mars
Rain wouldn't matter, riding in our car
The streetlights like planets, the headlights like stars

Adeline picked up the pace, plucking at the strings, thumping on the body of her guitar, while I sat rigid. I was hot. I was cold. I'd been struck through the heart by lightning. She'd written this song with my words from the balcony. The message couldn't have been clearer. The kiss had not been an accident.

> *Rain's stopped, but the clouds won't go away*
> *Sun shines, but it's never here to stay*
> *I'm waiting for you to come around*
> *I worry you don't like what you've found*

> *Wish I could be wherever you are*
> *Whether it's Michigan, whether it's Mars*
> *Rain wouldn't matter, riding in our car*
> *The streetlights like planets, the headlights like stars*

> *I'm waiting for you, I'm waiting for you, I'm waiting for you to come around. . . .*

The whole hall was clapping along, except for me.

No wonder Adeline had been hurt. I'd been blaming Olivia's jealousy for the distance between us, but I'd never stood up to her—and why? Was our friendship so fragile? Sure, I wanted Olivia to be happy, but what about me? Didn't I deserve to be happy, too? And if Olivia was really my best friend, wouldn't she want me to be?

Oh. The realization sank in my stomach. I knew I was unhappy, and why, but did Olivia? I'd hidden so much from her the past week and a half, pretending everything was fine. I'd said *I'm okay* a hundred times—every time she'd asked. I'd never given her a chance to understand.

As the lights came up after the show, I turned to Olivia. "We need to talk."

She raised her eyebrows. "You realize how ominous that sounds."

"Sorry," I said. "You don't need to be worried. I don't think."

"Comforting," Olivia said. "Okay. Let's talk. But when?"

"After lights-out. After the others are asleep. We can go to the fire circle."

My stomach somersaulted as I lay in the darkness later waiting for Toni's and Shauna's breathing to slow. Olivia and I had agreed not to talk after we got into bed, so the conversation lost steam quickly. When I could no longer hear voices murmuring across the campsite, I whispered Olivia's name. We ducked out from our netting and padded out of the tent, not bothering with our shoes. The earth was cool under my feet and dusted with soft, dry leaves.

We sat on the same log bench. I leaned over and hugged my knees. Adeline's song had given me a shot of bravery, but was it enough to get me through the things I needed to say?

Olivia waited for a long moment before saying, "It's kind of cold out here, Mel."

It was. I'd thought my shivering was just nerves, but in the woods, in the dark, it was chilly—and we were only wearing our pajamas. "I have to tell you something," I said.

"Yeah," Olivia said. "I kind of got that." Her voice softened. "Is it about your parents?"

"No," I said. "But since you mentioned it, there's something I need to tell you about them, too." I wrung the hem of my pajamas, twisting it back and forth, back and forth. It grew damp in my palms.

Olivia reached out a hand and took one of mine. "It's okay," she said. "I'm listening."

"It's been a hard couple of weeks," I said.

Olivia squeezed. "I know."

"First the divorce. And then coming here, when I didn't want to. And suddenly you had this crush on Noel and were always with him."

"I'm sorry," Olivia said. "I *was* sort of awful. And he totally wasn't worth it. But Melly—I told you if you needed me, I'd be there."

"I was doing fine, mostly," I said. "I was making new friends, too. I was having fun."

"Then what happened?"

Noel ditched you? Adeline kissed me? David tried?

"My dad told me why they're getting divorced," I blurted.

Olivia's eyes grew wide. "He did? So what's the big reason? Is it an affair?"

I shrugged. "There is no big reason. He says they just fell out of love."

"That's it?" Olivia said. "Well . . . well, that's not a very satisfying explanation."

"Right?" Her reaction was so much like my own that I giggled—but I choked on it. Tears welled in my eyes. I pulled a sleeve over my wrist and wiped my face. "He says they're still friends. Couldn't they stay friends in the same house? Did they even stop to think how I'd feel?"

"Oh, Melly." Olivia let go of my hand, but only to put her arm around my shoulders. "Trust me, I want to beat up your mom and dad for making you feel this way. But they're good people. I'm pretty sure they feel terrible right now."

"They don't sound like it in their letters," I said. "Mom's redoing the bathroom."

"Yes, because redoing the bathroom is a sure sign someone is feeling fantastic," Olivia said. We both giggled this time, and then we laughed harder at the giggle.

That's when I said, "Adeline kissed me."

Olivia clapped her hands to her mouth. "What? What do you mean she kissed you?"

I blushed. "She kissed me. On Sunday. On the HydroBlaster."

"The Hydro-*what*?"

"This ride at Michigan's Adventure. We were sitting in the dark, on this raft, waiting to go down the water slide. And it just sort of happened."

"No way. Kisses do not just sort of happen."

I shrugged, and even though things with Adeline were totally weird right now, the memory put a stupid grin on my face. Whatever happened next, nothing could undo that kiss.

"Well." Olivia seemed at a loss for words. "Did you want her to? What was it like?"

"Um." I fidgeted. I wanted her to know the truth, but I wished she could just *know* without me having to explain it. "It was like a total surprise. But . . . not a bad surprise."

She shook her head. "Oh my God. Melly, are you gay?"

"I don't know!" I said. My crush on Arjit had been real, even if it wasn't as deep. But the past two weeks had been filled with surprises. There'd be more around the bend. How was I supposed to know what would happen? "It was only one kiss, Olivia."

"But if you liked it—"

"Would it matter to you? If I was?"

"I don't know. I don't think so. I mean . . . for crying out loud, you're my best friend! Nothing's going to change that."

"I know," I said, believing it. "And you're mine."

"My best friend got her first kiss," Olivia said, shaking her head. "Melly, I can't believe you beat me."

I nudged her in the ribs. "That's not true. Remember Stella's party."

"That didn't count. That was on a dare. You got a real kiss."

"I didn't know it was a race."

"I didn't either! But now that I've lost, I'm feeling pretty low." She grinned ruefully. "Look. If you're happy, I'm happy. 'K?"

"'K," I said, but my smile faded. I took a deep breath. "The thing is, I'm not. Since it happened, Adeline and I have barely talked. First I thought what happened was maybe an accident, and then you were mad at me, and then I said some things she took the wrong way, and it's turned into a big mess. But I want to fix things."

"Oh, Mel," said Olivia. "I wish I'd known. I would've been so much nicer to her."

"You weren't completely wrong," I said. "I've only known her a week and a half. I've known you my whole life. On Sunday, all I wanted was to be with her, and I left you behind."

She exhaled, her bangs lifting from her forehead. "All right, yes, that was crappy. And I still would've gotten mad at you. But maybe I would've understood better. Maybe I would've been happy for you instead of jealous. I would've known you weren't leaving me for good."

My heart broke at the idea, and so did my voice. "I could never."

My best friend put her arms around me, a full-on hug this time, cradling my feelings as if they were her own.

twenty-four

"I told Olivia everything," I said to Adeline the second I walked into practice.

Her eyes went wide. "And?"

Caleb and David pushed through the door with their instruments, and Donna clapped her hands. "All right, people. We're at T minus forty-eight hours, and it's time for the training wheels to come off. Show me we haven't been wasting our time for the past week and a half."

"Let's talk after," I said. Adeline nodded.

David pulled the tie-dyed bandanna out of his bass case and wrapped it around his head. "I hope it's okay if I wear this," he mumbled.

"Of course," I said as casually as I could. "That's why I gave it to you."

We seemed to have agreed, without saying as much, to pretend nothing had happened between us. I'd be lying if I said it didn't feel weird to look into the eyes of the boy who'd tried to kiss me on the worst of all possible days, but practice went much better all the same.

Donna stopped us a few minutes early. "Two days, and you'll be onstage in front of hundreds of people. Whatever was off yesterday, you seem to have gotten over the hump. But you still need to finalize your set list and choose a name."

"I like our version of 'Enter Sandman,'" Adeline said.

"All right." Donna jotted it on the chalkboard. "What else?"

"I guess we could do 'I Knew You Were Trouble,'" Caleb said grudgingly. "As long as we do the metal version."

"Great. There's room for one more," Donna said. "What'll it be?"

That's when the arguing began. Caleb wanted "Pulse of the Maggots." Adeline wanted "Landslide." Angry voices collided in the cabin's cramped quarters.

Donna interrupted. "Melly. David. What do you think?"

"Either would be fine with me," I said, squirming. I think Donna was hoping I'd say "Rebel Girl," and I sort of wanted to. But something stopped me. Maybe I didn't want to jump in the middle of the argument. Or maybe I still wasn't ready to own it.

Sure enough, Donna looked disappointed. "Well, unless you're planning on playing the mash-up to end all mash-ups, you need to pick one," she said.

I suppose it was too much to expect David to rescue me. Sure enough, he'd pulled off the bandanna and was rolling it around his fingers. His hair hid his eyes. Everyone else watched me expectantly. "Um," I said. "What if we did an original?"

Everyone stared at me like a squid was coming out of my mouth.

Donna's eyebrows rocketed. "An original," she repeated. "As in, something you wrote? Well. This is news."

It was news to me, too. Why had I said it?

"But you don't write—" Adeline started, but stopped herself.

"You've got to be kidding," Caleb said. "When are we supposed to learn a new song?"

"Caleb makes a fair point, Melly," Donna said. "Do you have charts for us?"

I shouldn't have said anything. I didn't have a song for the band! I barely had an inkling. I'd never written a song in my life. But ever since my parents told me about the divorce, I'd been wondering how to make them hear my side of the story. What better time than the end-of-camp show, when they'd be a captive audience? They couldn't brush me off with a full band backing me up and the sound system cranked to eleven.

I swallowed. "I'll have them by practice tomorrow. And if I don't, or everyone hates it, then David should pick something."

"We can't seriously be considering this," Caleb said.

"What," said Adeline, "are you saying you're not up to the challenge? Personally, I think we should go for it. David, back me up." It was more of an order than a request.

He blushed and stared at the floor. "It's fine with me."

I felt a burst of gratitude and guilt. Adeline was standing up for me when I'd gone so long not standing up for her.

"Okay," Donna said. "This is your band, and you call the shots. Melly—" I forced myself to meet her gaze. It wasn't critical or concerned, as I'd expected. She looked almost proud. "I'll be very interested to see what you have for us."

Me, too, Donna. Me, too.

"Anyway, time's up for today. Bring your ideas for a band name to practice tomorrow."

Adeline waited outside Trolltunga for me. It was the first time in so long we'd been alone together. Instantly my stomach was a tangled cat's cradle. But the time for chickening out had passed. "Will you sit with me at lunch?" I asked.

"Do you want me to?" She sounded skeptical. "Will Olivia be okay with it?"

"I think so." After our talk last night, I certainly hoped so.

"How'd she react?" Adeline said. "You know, when you told her?"

I laughed a little. "She was surprised."

She laughed, too. "Which is . . . not surprising."

"And she was sorry."

"Sorry? What for?"

"Sorry she wasn't nicer. She didn't know. Which was my fault. She thought—"

"I was trying to steal you," Adeline finished, rolling her eyes.

"I guess it sounds stupid," I said.

Olivia and I had seen other kids ditch their friends for a more popular group or something, and we'd sworn it would never happen to us. Our friendship was too strong. But honestly, this summer was the first time the threat had seemed real. Now I knew how scary and horrible it was. The fear didn't seem stupid at all.

"Anyway," Adeline said. "If she's nice to me, I'll be nice to her. I always figured someone would have to be pretty great to be best friends with you. But Melly . . ."

When she said my name, I felt as warm and melty as a dab of butter on a slice of hot toast. "Yeah?"

"What you said about having written a song?" Her forehead crinkled. "When did that happen?"

"Well, that's the tricky part," I said. "It hasn't, yet."

Adeline let out a delighted, incredulous *ha!* "Just when I think I'm starting to know you."

"You are," I promised. "But I need your help. What are you doing this afternoon?"

Everyone was on their best behavior at lunch. Olivia was extra polite, asking Adeline questions about her music and where she was from and nodding enthusiastically at every answer. When I told her Adeline and I needed to work on band stuff, she said, "Absolutely not a problem!" She was trying a little too hard, but I didn't care. Things were so much better already.

Adeline picked me up at my tent after B-flat. "Where do you want to go?" she asked. "Meadow? Library? Practice stall?"

"Do you think a canoe would be too tricky?" It had been so peaceful on the lake, so far away from everything else.

Adeline thought it over. "Possibly. But I have another idea. Got your notebook?"

"I don't have a notebook," I said. Then I remembered

what I did have. I went back and got the stationery and pen Mom had packed me.

Down at Joan Jetty, Adeline said to Skip, "One johnboat and two life jackets, please."

The johnboat was blunt at the ends and painted green. We helped Skip carry it to the water's edge and plugged a long, wooden oar into the lock on either side. Adeline sat on the center bench with the oars, facing Skip and me. I climbed into the nearest seat. Skip pushed us off. Adeline dipped the oars into the rippled glass water and rowed us backward from shore. The oars creaked and splashed.

"Not as fast as a canoe," she said, "but it's more stable. Plus, I don't have to stare at the back of your head the whole time."

I said, "But now you have to stare at my face."

"You say that like it's a bad thing." Her smile made my stomach flip. "So this song you're writing . . ."

"I haven't even started," I admitted. "I have some ideas but nothing written."

"Ideas are a start," Adeline said. "Why don't you write them down?"

"They're probably stupid. They'd probably make a terrible song."

She shook her head. "That's just fear talking. Nothing's scarier than a blank page."

Nothing? What about skydiving or car accidents

or war? But I remembered standing at the edge of the dock, inching out over the water to dive. I remembered teetering at the peak of the Shivering Timbers, holding my breath, not knowing when the wheels would release. It wasn't the doing that was the scariest part. It was the anticipation. I picked up my pen.

"Write three words," Adeline said. "That's something Poppy has us do in songwriting workshop when we're feeling stuck. Three words. Any three. And me? I'll keep rowing."

I uncapped my pen and held it over the stationery balanced on my knees. The cheery yellow suns around the margins were completely wrong for my thoughts. I lowered the pen and wrote lightly, afraid to press the tip against the paper, *Parents*.

It looked harmless enough. I pressed harder, adding, *Divorce*.

Better, but it still didn't get to the heart of the matter. I wrote in capital letters, hard enough to make an impression on the sheet below, *MAD*.

But that still wasn't it. Mad was what little kids got when they didn't get a pack of M&M's in the grocery aisle, or when someone else snatched the toy they were playing with. What I felt was way bigger than that. Adeline was still rowing, not even looking at me, so I set my pen to the paper again.

There was no warning. That's the worst part. It's not like I expected them to ask my opinion, because obviously I would have said don't do it. But afterward it's like I still don't get to have an opinion. They expect me to go to camp and act like everything is normal. They expect me to come home and say okay, I get it, everything is fine. Well, it's not fine! I may have to live with their decision . . . but I do NOT have to be okay with it. No matter how much they may want me to be the quiet little Melly they're used to. I am FURIOUS and HEARTBROKEN and I am NOT going to pretend I'm not. They can't tell me how to feel.

I stopped, my hand cramped. I'd used up three sheets of stationery without realizing it, flipping from one to the next when it filled up. My pen hovered over the page, but after a moment I realized I'd said what I needed to say. I capped the pen and set it on my lap.

Adeline settled the dripping oars in the boat. "That was way more than three words."

I barked a little laugh. "Yeah. I guess it was."

"Can I read it? Or can you read it to me?" she asked.

I didn't think I could, not without crying, so I passed the pages to her. She smoothed them out and read them silently. When she was done she returned them.

"If you had to summarize this," she said, "in ten

words or less, what would you say? What would you tell your parents?"

"Easy," I said. "Just take the last sentence. It's all there."

Adeline nodded. "That's your song."

I stared at her. "My song," I echoed.

"Sure."

"'They can't tell me how to feel'? That's not remotely poetic."

"Poetry, schmoetry. This is the cake. The rest is just frosting. Now, scoot over."

I made room on my bench. The metal was hot where I hadn't been sitting. Between that and the sudden nearness of Adeline, I was roasting.

Her knee brushed against mine as she pulled the blank stationery and pen out of my hands, and there was that electricity again, the pulse zipping out of my heart and through my limbs and into Adeline and back again. When it came back, it felt different, as if it were carrying something of her. Something different. Something wonderful.

Adeline hunched beside me, scribbling words. They weren't neat or pretty like the stationery. She crossed out and drew little circles and arrows, all the while asking me questions, listening to my answers, and asking more questions. We tossed rhymes back and forth. She hummed snatches of melody. I tapped rhythms on my knees. Her song the night before had been so pretty, so polished. Had it started like this, dull and pitted and heavy, spending hours in the tumbler before its pattern shone through?

"This still isn't remotely poetic," I said when we were through.

Adeline rolled her eyes. "Give yourself a break. It's your first song."

"It's literally the most literal song ever."

"Okay. But does it say what you want it to say?"

I sighed. "I guess so. I mean, I don't think it could be any more direct than it is."

"Then it's fine. Now, what do you think about it going like this?" She sang a few bars, combining lyrics, beat, and melody just like that.

"How do you do it?" I asked, shaking my head.

"Poppy's workshops help. But it's like anything else. You keep doing it, you get better."

"No," I said. "I mean, how are you so sure? Of everything? All the time?"

My words hung in the steamy summer air. Adeline blew out her breath. "More practice I guess. And a lot of faking."

I waited. The boat, our tiny island, bobbed in the breeze.

"Here's what I think," Adeline said. "When your dad is sick and getting a little worse every day, you have to think positive. You'd go crazy if you didn't. Especially having two little brothers. They don't get it. They don't get how serious things are, because things have been like this since they can remember. They didn't see the *before* to know how bad the *after* is."

I didn't know what to say. I put my hand over hers and squeezed.

"I guess I'm trying to say I know better than to expect everything will turn out all right in the end. Some things just don't. But even when I can't expect, I still hope."

"When you kissed me—"

"I'm sorry," Adeline said. "I should've asked you first. I was so sure you were feeling something, too, that it wasn't just me. Maybe I let my hoping turn into expecting. Or maybe I was afraid if I asked, you'd say no. Either way it was wrong."

I thought of David, who hadn't asked either. "I probably would've been too surprised to say yes or no," I said, "but I guess you're right. Asking would've been the right thing to do."

"It's more than that," Adeline said. "I knew you were going through something with your family. I should've respected that. I told you, when I come here—it's like my vacation, right? My little paradise in the woods? But the first year I came, my mom basically dragged me, kicking and screaming."

"How come?"

"It wasn't long after my dad was diagnosed," said Adeline. "We'd known something wasn't right for a while, and the pieces had finally fallen into place. But I didn't understand how it worked, that he'd gradually get worse over a matter of years, little bit by little bit. I was positive I'd come home from school one day and he'd have dropped dead. It was getting to the point where I wouldn't eat and could barely sleep. Which of course only stressed my parents out more. They decided the only way to calm me down was to get me out of the situation entirely."

"So they sent you here," I said.

Adeline nodded. "I didn't even play guitar back then, but Mom saw a cashier at the food co-op wearing a Camp Rockaway shirt and thought it sounded like the perfect place to put me. I couldn't believe they wanted to send me away. The way I saw it, they needed my help, and what if Dad got worse while I was gone? It was only two weeks, but it was awful. At first, anyway."

"What happened?"

"Much as I hated to admit it, they were right. Getting away was exactly what I needed. It gave me a chance to focus on myself for a change, instead of being so focused on my family. By the time camp was over, I still wanted to come home. But I also knew I wanted to come back every summer, for as long as I could."

"And here you are," I said, not sure what all this had to do with me.

"Melly, meeting you—" Adeline said. Her cheeks flushed dark rose. "I've had crushes here before. You know Yasmina? If you think Olivia had it bad for Noel, you should've seen me last summer."

"You're kidding!" I said. I'd known Adeline and Yasmina were close, but I'd always assumed they were plain old friends.

"Not even a little bit," Adeline said. "It didn't help that she was a year older. I basically worshipped her. It's embarrassing to think about. When she and this Bass Cliff guy started hanging out, and I realized she was only ever going to like me as a friend, I was devastated."

"Did she know?"

"She's never said anything, which is fine with me. Things are better this way." Adeline shrugged. "But you—you're the first person I thought might really like me back. So I went after you, full steam ahead, only thinking about what I wanted. Not about what you might need."

"Look," I said, inching closer. "Whatever you think you did wrong, I forgive you, okay? And I do like you back. And I want you to kiss me."

In the movies, everyone closes their eyes when they kiss. I didn't want to. Not just because I was afraid of missing Adeline's lips and getting her ear instead. I didn't want to miss anything about the moment, from the clear bright sky over the deep blue lake, to our little johnboat aimlessly floating, to the blue and black damselfly resting its wings on the blade of an oar.

I leaned forward, eyes locked on Adeline's so there would be no question what it meant, and kissed her. And when our lips touched, I could've sworn the world was spinning backward, the johnboat had capsized after all, and we were tumbling headfirst into the water.

But there was the smell of sunscreen on Adeline's cheeks, her chapped lips, both soft and rough, against mine, and the sun setting us on fire.

"Okay then," Adeline said shakily, pulling back. "Okay."

"Okay," I said.

twenty-five

At band practice, Donna wasted no time. "Okay, Melly. Don't keep us in suspense. Where's this song you have for us?"

Adeline had shown me the chart at breakfast. "I finished it last night after lights-out," she'd whispered, so Olivia and the others couldn't hear. "Had to hide my flashlight because Poppy kept catching me. I'll make copies after breakfast."

She'd written "How to Feel" in block letters at the top, then the melody line and chords and lyrics. It was so unlike the chicken scratch on that ridiculous sunshine paper. It felt real.

After shuffling around the cabin, handing everyone a copy, I sat behind the drums, staring at my hands. Donna hummed the melody, tapping her hand against her thigh. "I think I get the idea," she said, "but why don't you sing it through for us?"

I froze. My imagination had jumped to everyone singing together, everyone else's voices drowning out mine—the way I was used to. The way, I had to admit, I sometimes preferred. But of course, we didn't have a recording for everyone to listen to. That was my job.

"I could sing it for you, if you want," Adeline said.

It would've been so easy to say yes, and part of me sure wanted to. But it was my song. I had to do this for myself. "No," I said, "I'm okay."

Adeline nodded. "I'll back you up if you change your mind."

Hands trembling, I lifted my sticks and clicked them together. *One—two—one, two, three, four.* Adeline came in on guitar. Then I started singing, grateful we'd kept the melody super simple and smack in the middle of my lousy range. I didn't even have to sing, really. I could almost talk my way through the lyrics, pretending I was Lou Reed. No one would accuse him of having a beautiful voice, but he was a legend. That was one of the great things about rock, I was coming to accept. You could have the worst voice in the world, and it didn't matter as long as you sang like you meant it.

Of course, I wasn't Lou Reed. My voice shook along with my hands, and I stumbled more than once, even though I was playing at a turtle's pace. I kept my eyes on Adeline's, occasionally glancing at the chart, more for security's sake than out of necessity. We'd sung all the way back into shore yesterday. I knew the song by heart.

When I mustered the guts to look at the others, Donna was bobbing her head to the beat and even mouthing the words. David swayed in time. Even Caleb's scowl had smoothed out.

"It's rough," Donna said, after Adeline strummed the final jangling chord and I rolled my sticks to a finish and struck my crash cymbal one last time. "And I'd want to increase the tempo. But it's off to a strong start, Melly. Well done."

Somehow I knew those two little words—*well done*—were the highest praise Donna could offer, and they were all the more significant for their simplicity. I nodded back at her. Adeline believed in me, and now so did Donna. "Guys?" I asked tentatively.

"It'd rock more with electric," Caleb said. Call me crazy, but I think it was a compliment.

"David?"

David brushed his hair out of his eyes. "Yeah. I think it's pretty good."

"Terrific," Donna said. "In that case, you four have the rest of class to make something out of this song and practice the rest of your set."

In some ways this practice was harder than any of the ones before, because it was our last. If we weren't ready for showtime by the end, we'd embarrass ourselves in front of our families tomorrow and, worse, our fellow musicians. But in some ways it was also the easiest practice, because after two weeks we worked together better than ever.

Yeah, David and I weren't as tight a rhythm section as Olivia and I were. And Caleb rushed and noodled all over the neck of his guitar even when the song did not call for noodling. But it sounded better than I'd ever hoped for. By the end, we were as ready as we could be without another week of practice.

"Okay, people," Donna said when her watch beeped. "It's time to pack it in, but this is the time I'm supposed to take a few minutes to tell you how hard you've worked, what a great team you've become, how you should totally come back to Camp Rockaway next year, yada yada yada."

"Flattery," Adeline said.

"You think I, of all people, would exaggerate?" said Donna. "You *have* worked hard, and you've become a great team, considering the circumstances."

Everyone exchanged a glance. "What's that supposed to mean?" Caleb said.

"Yeah," said Adeline, "considering what circumstances?"

"You might have noticed that your musical interests are . . . diverse. We match people up as much as we can, based on what you tell us at your audition. So we end up with a ska band, a power pop band, a metal band or five. But sometimes we have one too many metalheads or Taylor Swift fans. Or someone who doesn't care what genre they play, as long as there's good lyrics. Or someone who just wants to make some noise." Donna's eyes met mine, and the corners of her mouth quirked up.

"You're saying we're the leftovers," Caleb said flatly.

"That's one way of putting it," Donna said.

"And you threw us together to see what would happen. Like a science experiment."

"Or a smoothie," Adeline said.

Donna shrugged. "Sometimes it works out. Sometimes it doesn't. You four had a rocky start, but you pushed through. Play tomorrow the way you did today, and you can be proud. I'll be proud, too."

"We still don't have a name, though," Adeline said.

An idea popped into my head, and I grinned. "Yes, we do."

"We do?"

"Sure," I said. "Caleb said it. We're the Leftovers."

For once there was no arguing. Everyone agreed it was perfect.

Dear Melly,
 The bathroom is Perfectly Peach! Or imperfectly. I'm

not going to quit my job to become a painter anytime soon. It will take some getting used to, but I'm already enjoying the results. It's so fresh, so peaceful. As soon as the paint cures, I'm taking a good, long bubble bath.

Your dad told me he tried to explain things to you. I wish he'd waited until we could all sit down together, but too late now. We'll talk more when you get home.

Speaking of which, we decided to drive up together to pick you up. There's no sense wasting the gas. I don't want you to get the wrong idea when you see us. We're not getting back together. But we're trying to be kind to each other.

At this point I'm not holding my breath for a letter from you, but that's okay. All I really want is to see you and give you a great big hug.

Lots of love,

Mom

I leaned over the edge of my bed and crammed my arm as far into my suitcase as I could reach. My fingers brushed crumpled paper. I drew out the letters, one after another, until they littered my lap like crinkly snowballs. I didn't read them again, didn't even smooth them out. I cupped them in my hands and thought.

Tomorrow I'd ride home in the back seat of my parents' car, and in some ways life would return to its pre-camp state. But in the biggest way possible, things would never be the same again. If my parents were hoping I'd spent the past two weeks meditating and finding inner peace through the power of music, they were out of luck. Melly Mouse had left the building.

I split the rest of the day between my two favorite people at Camp Rockaway. It meant missing yet another of Damon's percussion workshops, but that was okay. There was always next year.

After B-flat, Olivia and I ran through her group's set list. I felt bad her band had become such a mess, what with the Noel drama. I guess, right or wrong, Candace never did apologize. But I was glad I could be there for Olivia.

Next we headed to the lake, where Olivia hung out with the other sunbathers while Adeline and I borrowed a johnboat. We rowed out until the campers at the beach were only colored dots, the lifeguards specks of red on the distant white dock. Then we sat on one bench and held hands and kissed and only talked when we felt like it.

Randomly, a question occurred to me. "You know this morning, when Donna was talking about how the four of us were leftovers?"

"Yeah?"

"Well, obviously Caleb's the extra metalhead. And if I had to guess, you're the person who said you like any genre as long as the song has good lyrics."

"Right you are," said Adeline.

"Then who's into Taylor Swift?"

"You mean it's not you?"

I gave her a look. She cracked up. "Guess not! It must be David."

"Do you think so?"

"Who else could it be?" she asked.

"Until today, I thought it was you. Caleb sure did."

"And David didn't 'fess up." Adeline grinned. "I figured if Caleb was going to give someone hell, it might as well be me. Besides which, I do like Taylor Swift. Girl's got talent. Anyway, that solves another mystery."

"What's that?" I asked.

"By process of elimination, you came to Camp Rockaway to make some noise," she said. "Well, congratulations, Melly. After tomorrow? Mission accomplished."

At firebowl, I sat squeezed on a bench between Olivia and Adeline. I leaned into Adeline a little and felt her do the same. I didn't think anyone would notice, but Toni said, "I guess we were wrong about you and David, huh, Melly?"

"Um, yeah," I said, cheeks flaming. "You could say that."

"Just as well," said Toni. "You two make an even cuter couple."

"Don't say *cute*," Shauna said. "It's infantilizing."

"What should I say? *Pretty*? *Beautiful*? *Drop-dead gorgeous*?"

Shauna winced harder at every word, and the rest of us laughed.

"How about *bold*?" I said. I was sort of kidding, but sort of not. Because when it came down to it, there was no better word for the way Adeline made me feel.

"*Bold*," Adeline repeated. "I like it."

"Oo, Adeline likes it!" Olivia said. "But does Shauna approve?"

"Shauna wholeheartedly approves," said Shauna.

We sang, a hundred of us and then some, our voices overlaying the chorus of frogs and crickets, toads and sheep. As the sun sank low, Olivia nudged me. "We still haven't led a song."

"Damon said we're slowing things down," I said. "He won't want a drummer now."

"If anyone can do quiet on drums, it's you," Olivia said. "Come on." She pulled me down the side aisle before I could protest. I threw a helpless look backward at Adeline. She gave me a big smile, her braces glinting in the firelight, and a thumbs-up.

"We want to lead a song," Olivia told Damon in a whisper. "A song about friendship."

"I'm all about friendship," he said. "Do you have a particular song in mind?"

"Yes, we do," Olivia said, "but it's a surprise."

Once, not knowing would've made me panic. Now, I nodded in agreement. I trusted Olivia. More than that, I trusted myself. As the notes of the previous song died away, we walked in front of the fire, Olivia with a borrowed guitar and me with a djembe.

"Hey," Olivia said. "We're Olivia and Melly from Treble Cliff. We've been friends almost all our lives, so, not to brag, but we're kind of an authority on friendship. And if you asked me what keeps us together, I'd tell you the answer's in this song. Key of C. Please join in."

She counted us in, and I started playing, hesitantly thumping the skin of the drum, slapping the rim where the skin met the body, still not knowing what the song was. Then she started singing "Lean on Me." She was right. It was perfect as ever. Perfect for old friends, perfect for new—so long as they were true.

Soon everyone was singing. Other campers and counselors joined us and played along. In the audience, people put their arms around each other's shoulders and swayed.

For the first time in my life, surrounded in that spiral of firelight and my fellow musicians and the trees and the first stars peeking out of the deep, dark blue, I got a sense of what it's like to have a family you weren't born into. It wasn't like I was disowning my parents or anything. I might be angry, but it came out of love. But this—this was something different, bigger, something I'd discovered on my own, and that made it extra special.

There were people at camp who drove me crazy, and people I'd quickly grown to love, and one person especially who—well, I didn't have words worthy to explain how Adeline made me feel. She smiled at me from the audience, and my heart fizzed and sparkled like a firecracker. But at the end of it everyone was here for the music. Music was the ribbon that wove us together, and as we sang, I felt myself pulled tighter and tighter into the fabric.

I couldn't wiggle loose if I tried.

twenty-six

Saturday. I woke short of breath, as if I'd been climbing a rocky, steep hill and had just now paused to take in the view. Today was the show. Today I'd see my parents. I'd leave Adeline. I'd go home. I wished I could go back to yesterday and press repeat.

After breakfast we packed up our belongings, stuffing our suitcases full of dirty laundry, taking down our mosquito netting, and rolling up our sleeping bags. We carried everything down the slippery path to the foot of Treble Cliff. The ranger would come by with his truck to pick it all up and take it to the parking lot.

There was no time for last-minute practice, no time for soccer or arts and crafts, swimming or boating. Besides passing the toast and eggs at breakfast, there hadn't even been time for me to see Adeline. We made one final hike to the lodge. Campers who needed to pick up their instruments for the last time did so. I carried my stick bag on my shoulder. Even though the big show was still ahead, camp felt over.

Inside the dining hall was chaos. Parents stood in clusters with toddlers clinging to their shins, comparing notes on their children. Little kids raced around shrieking. Older siblings hung against the wall, looking bored. Right away, Olivia spotted her parents and grandparents and sisters. I couldn't help it: I started scanning the throng for my own family. My own family, such as it was. I guess it was instinct.

Adeline broke into a run at the sight of a tall woman with a cloud of black curls and a man in a wheelchair. He pushed himself out of his chair and held out his arms, and she fell into them. Two little boys piled at their legs. An older woman with a face as wrinkled and brown as a walnut scooped them against her. I felt a pang. Just like that, Adeline no longer belonged to Camp Rockaway, or to me. She belonged to her family.

Then there were my own parents. Even though I'd spent the past two weeks alternating between being furious at them and pretending they didn't exist, that tension went suddenly slack. Dad had grown a ridiculous beard, all streaked with white like a skunk's tail, and Mom was made up more than usual. But their grins were the same grins I knew, splitting their faces in two, they were so wide. I stepped up, prepared to stand like a telephone pole, stiff and splintery. But it was only a moment before I softened in their arms and hugged them back.

"Oh, it is so good to see you!" Mom whispered. "Longest two weeks of my life."

"Your mom and I agreed, you're never allowed away from home again," Dad said.

I didn't bother pointing out that *home* didn't mean what it used to.

The lights in the hall flashed, and up onstage Damon tapped the mic. "Attention, rock stars and rock star families. Thank you all for joining us at Camp Rockaway this summer. It's been a challenging and productive couple of weeks. Now it's time to see—or should I say, hear—the fruits of everyone's labor. Please have a seat, and we'll get started."

The grown-ups moved toward the rows of chairs. There weren't enough, so all the kids had to sit on the floor in front. I scrambled into an empty spot between Olivia and Adeline as the houselights dimmed.

"All right," Damon said, "let's give it up for our first band of the day: the Moose Farts!"

The younger bands played two songs each. There was a short break for refreshments, and the second set began. I whispered my friends good luck beforehand.

Clapped and cheered them onstage. Hugged them and clasped their hands afterward. Nobody's band was perfect, but you wouldn't have known it from the way they glowed as they returned to their seats. Even Olivia's band managed to click.

The Leftovers came last in the second act, naturally. Even having spent the past hour and a half watching all the bands who'd come before, I was surprised how magical it felt when Damon—goofy, pot-bellied Damon—came out and said, "Adeline, Caleb, David, and Melly, with their unique fusion of punk, pop, and metal. Please welcome the Leftovers!"

The crowd cheered as we jogged onstage under the pink and blue lights. I adjusted my seat and the tension on the pedals. My bandmates plugged in and quickly tuned. There was no time to stall. Ten minutes—on and off. I imagined trapdoors opening beneath us if we went over our time limit. The thought was actually comforting. No matter what happened, in ten minutes it'd be history.

"Thanks, everyone," Adeline said, her breath puffing against the mic. She, of course, didn't sound remotely nervous. "We are indeed the Leftovers, and we're going to start out with a little Taylor Swift, as you've never heard her before!"

This was it. I clicked my sticks together, and we

launched into our rapid-fire, head-slamming rendition of "I Knew You Were Trouble."

Right away, things felt off. In the cavernous dining hall, my bandmates spread across the stage instead of crowded around me, I felt disconnected. They shimmered at the edge of my vision. In spite of the monitors, which my buzzing ears told me were cranked, the sound seemed to come from miles away, not from their fingers and lips.

My brain worked frantically as Caleb snarled the first verse. Was I rushing? Was Caleb? Was I letting him? What about David? Were we in sync, or had I lost him? Was I supposed to put a fill there? In practice, I put a fill there. Would anyone know the difference? I was running through a dark wood, stumbling and staggering to keep my feet under me.

Then all of our voices joined for the chorus, and everything changed. My panic evaporated. The path was clear. My hands unclenched, my shoulders settled back, and I sang—no, bellowed—the words. The drums bellowed with me. My racing pulse caught its stride.

I shivered as Adeline threw back her head and wailed. Only the tie-dyed bandanna kept David's face visible as he swung his head in time to the music. Caleb was jumping all over the place. If he hadn't been plugged in, he probably would've dived off the stage and tried to crowd surf. He wasn't the only one. Down in front, kids were whipping their hair. Even the adults were standing, if only so they could see.

This is what it feels like to be a rock star, if only for ten minutes.

School concerts were so civilized. They were all about playing the notes exactly as they appeared on the page. Screw civilization. Screw perfection. Donna was right: rock was way more fun when I embraced my inner rebel. I laughed as we emerged from the final chorus. I beat what Grandma Schiff would've called the living daylights out of those drums. Caleb strummed the final chords with an arm so long he almost touched his toes. Ears ringing with applause, the four of us grinned at each other.

But there was no time to waste. Caleb introduced "Enter Sandman," and just as the audience was preparing to rock out again, Adeline surprised them by fingerpicking a delicate intro high on the neck of her acoustic. Then came her hushed, haunting vocals. Everyone sat in a hurry to listen. Cheering still filled the room when it was over, but it had a different quality—more thoughtful, somehow.

We did that. We'd changed them; we'd literally changed them. We weren't just musicians. We were magicians. I'd never felt so powerful.

And then it was my turn. My turn to talk. My turn to sing. My turn to lead.

It was time, finally, to send a letter to my parents.

I pulled my mic a couple of inches closer with a trembling hand. My voice shook, too, as I said, "Our last song is an original I wrote with Adeline. It's called 'How to Feel.' Please feel free to get up and dance."

The arrangement had come a long way. Caleb started this one alone, fast and bright—short bursts in a simple chord progression, no fancy finger work. A couple of bars later, the rest of us jumped in. The beat was cheerful, a beat made for tapping your toes as you did your math, for shaking your behind as you washed the dishes. I could see the audience begin nodding their heads in time. Ignoring the quiver in my voice, I leaned into the mic and sang.

Just as I'm waking up
You tell me you're breaking up
You've made up your mind, clear as day
Then you send me away
You wave good-bye and say
When I come back home, I'll be okay

But you can't tell me, you can't tell me, you can't tell me how to feel
You can't tell me, you can't tell me, you can't tell me how to feel

At the chorus, we switched from our happy dance vibe to—well, there's really no other way to put it: we screamed. We screamed, all of us together, and our instruments screamed with us. In front of the stage, kids leaped to their feet, jumping around and knocking into each other. It was a little scary, and for a second I thought the grown-ups would wade in and pull them apart, or the sound system would cut off and Damon would haul us off the stage.

But just when it seemed the scene might boil over, we got to the second verse. Everything was sunshine again.

You tell me don't be upset
But there's no way I'll forget
You broke two halves from our whole
You've made a big mistake
Fine, it's your choice to make
Still there's one thing you can't control

You can't tell me, you can't tell me, you can't tell me how to feel
You can't tell me, you can't tell me, you can't tell me how to feel

Out in the johnboat, I hadn't been sure how to end the song. Continue until our voices were hoarse whispers? Groove our way out? But Adeline had said, "Why not something completely different?" So we muted our instruments, and I sang the last two lines a cappella.

I've had two weeks to sing and play
But in case you wondered, I'm still not okay

Then it was over. The Leftovers made our final bow as the houselights came up. I followed my bandmates offstage as Damon came on to announce the intermission, and my friends piled on me with congratulations and hugs. Adeline took my hands, and we twirled in a triumphant circle. My heart bounced off the beams in the ceiling.

Donna slapped our hands. "Well done," she told us. "Very well done."

We'd played a good set, she meant. I wondered if she knew it was so much more for me.

She caught my eye and gave me a quick nod. *Yep. She definitely knows.*

I didn't look for my parents. I'd taken a tube of emotional toothpaste and given it a hard squeeze with both fists. There was no way any of that stuff was ever going back inside. I wanted to take a minute and enjoy how good I felt.

I didn't look for my parents, but I thought they'd come looking for me.

They didn't.

And they didn't.

And when I finally turned around and searched the room, they were nowhere to be seen.

twenty-seven

"What's wrong?" Olivia asked as I craned my neck.

"My parents. I don't know where they are."

"Oh no. Do you think they heard your song and . . ." She shook her head as if she didn't know how to finish the sentence.

I didn't either. I'd been so desperate to tell Mom and Dad how I felt. I'd barely thought about how they'd feel hearing it, about what they'd say or do. Now that I stopped to consider it, nothing good came to mind. What had I been thinking? I should've kept my mouth shut.

"Come on," Olivia said. "Let's split up. I'll go by the bathrooms. You go by the snacks."

The two of us set off in different directions, so much like the week before when we'd searched for Noel at the end of the dance. Our search was just as futile. We pushed through families of all sizes and configurations, but my parents were nowhere in the lodge. My throat

squeezed. They wouldn't have left me at Camp Rockaway; they couldn't have. But where had they gone?

"I'm going to check outside," I told Olivia.

"Want me to come with?"

"No. Thanks. They've got to be close by."

Olivia nodded. "I'll save your seat."

I pushed out the door of the lodge and blinked in the
sun. There were a few sets of parents taking a breather
out on the lawn. One father guiltily stubbed out his
cigarette when he saw me. But none of them was my
mom or dad. I scuffed through the grass, not knowing
where to go, rounding one corner of the building and
then another. Then there they were.

They sat in the grass, their backs to me. Dad's arm
was wrapped around Mom's shoulders. And I admit it:
I had a flash of hope that they'd woken from whatever
awful spell they'd been under. They'd realized they
were still in love after all, or something close enough to
it not to throw it away. My song had reversed the curse.
They were together.

Then I saw how under Dad's arm, Mom's shoulders
were hunched and shaking. Mom, who'd delivered the
news of the divorce without a single tear, who'd written
me one perky letter after another. Today I was the one
who'd broken something. I was the one with terrible
timing.

They'd driven all the way from Kalamazoo, together,

because they were my parents. They'd come to see my show, together, because it was supposed to be my special day. They'd come to pick me up, together, because in spite of everything, I was both of theirs.

Together.

I'd taken that togetherness and torn it into pieces. I'd trashed that togetherness like a rock star's hotel room, and it didn't feel one bit freeing anymore. It felt irresponsible. It felt like crap.

I trudged over. My hands flexed into fists, then released, flexed and released, as I tried to think what to say. But when I made it all the way over, all I could croak was, "Hi."

I expected Dad to glare at me. I expected Mom to cry all the harder. Instead, as they turned to look up at me, she was the first to smile. A watery, shaky smile, but a smile just the same. "Melly. Sunshine."

She fumbled in her handbag for a tissue and blew her nose. Dad stood and helped Mom up beside him. They hugged me—first Mom, then Dad. Their embraces had none of the fierce affection from earlier. This time they held me gingerly, as if they were afraid they'd break me. Or they were afraid I'd break them.

I didn't understand. Weren't they angry? Weren't they absolutely furious?

Or were they once again going to pretend everything was fine?

"We don't have to talk about this now," Mom said, as if she'd read my mind. "This is your day, sweetie."

I thought about it for the time it takes an acorn to fall. It was too late not to talk about it. The sky had already fallen. "When will we talk about it?" I said. "What if we always say we'll talk later, but we never do?"

"We will, Melly," Dad said.

"How can you say that?" I said. "If we'd talked a long time ago, maybe all of us could've fixed things before it was too late. Instead you waited until you'd already made up your minds." Suddenly I was the one who was crying.

"How many times have we told you?" Mom said. "It wasn't your fault. Not in the least."

I pushed them away. "Like I need to be reminded I have absolutely no control."

For a moment I thought about stalking away. I'd figure out where when I got there. Instead I turned and slumped in the grass, hugging my shins. My parents shuffled behind me. I pictured them speaking with their eyes, deciding what to do—twenty years' worth of silent language they'd invented together. So I wasn't surprised when, as one, they moved closer and sat, one on either side of me, not touching me. They waited.

The indistinct roar of conversation from the lodge grew frenzied as Damon announced the next act.

Wailing guitars, thumping drums, and bass so low it sent vibrations through the hill soon emanated from the windows.

I said, "Before you sent me here, you couldn't wait to talk about the divorce. Now you don't want to. Which is it?"

"That was our mistake," Mom said, at the same time as Dad said, "That was selfish."

"I believed everything I said two weeks ago," Mom said. "That it was better to get the truth out in the open so we could all begin healing. You know me, Melly. I hate letting things hang. I really did hope camp would take the sting off the news. But sending you off to cope with something this big on your own—that was completely unfair."

"She's right," said Dad. "Telling you was hard, but it was also a relief. At first I thought that meant it had been the right call. It took a while to realize that if my burden seemed lighter, it was because you were here, alone, carrying it. And then I felt terrible. I'm sorry, Melly."

They didn't say anything else. Were they waiting for me to forgive them? I wondered how often this happened, that parents actually apologized for the messed-up things they did. I supposed I should count myself lucky. Except I didn't feel lucky. Or forgiving.

"So are you happy now that you're apart?" I said harshly.

Dad rubbed his hand across his jaw. Two weeks without shaving, and the beard looked like it had always been there. "*Happy* isn't the right word," he said.

"Then why don't you come back?" I begged. "It's not too late."

"Doing what's necessary doesn't always make you feel better," Mom said, touching my arm. "Not right away."

"I think that's one difference between needing and wanting," Dad said. "Doing what you want feels good, at least in the short term. Telling you the news the way we did—we thought we needed to. We told ourselves we needed to. But we didn't. We just wanted to get it off our chests so we could start thinking about other things. We put our wants ahead of your needs. That's something parents should never do."

I had to hand it to him. He'd doubled down on his apology, and his watery blue eyes said he meant every word. But what good did that do?

I stared into the trees, avoiding my parents' anxious gazes. When I'd left a crying Olivia alone on field trip day? That had been me putting my wants ahead of her needs, and I'd been a rotten friend for doing it. And when I'd denied my feelings for Adeline because

I didn't want Olivia to be jealous? That had been me putting Olivia's wants ahead of my own needs, and it was a disaster, too. How was anyone supposed to figure out this stuff? It was depressing to think I could live another twenty-five years and still be clueless. I felt sorry for my hypothetical kids.

I looked at my mother, sunken into the ground, her round face blotchy. I looked at my father, who would've been quivering at the edge of his seat, if we'd been sitting in chairs instead of on a tickly grass slope. They were so obviously miserable, so obviously eager for me to relieve them of that misery, yet part of me didn't feel sorry for them one bit. I wanted to drag the whole thing into a long, tearful argument that looped around and around but never went anywhere because no matter what I said, things would never go back to the way they were before. That's what I wanted to do.

But I could also see they needed me to accept their apology. To finish out camp. To know they loved me. To trust things really would get better in time. And maybe, if I was being honest—maybe that's what I needed, too.

I took a deep breath and stood. "We should go back in so we can catch the end of the show."

"Melly, wait," Mom said. "We don't have to if you don't want to. We can stay out here and talk as long as you need."

"At least until they kick us out or demand another two weeks' tuition," Dad said.

"No, it's like you said," I said. "Talking can't fix things. Only time will help."

"Talking can help, too," Mom said.

"Later," I said firmly and began walking back to the lodge.

"Melly," Mom called, her voice breaking. I turned. She and Dad stood just feet apart, but I felt their distance like a chasm. Dad stepped toward me with open arms. Mom followed.

They wanted another hug? Seriously? I went back and let them squeeze me to a pulp. Maybe they didn't have each other anymore, not in the same way. But they still had me.

We stood in the back of the lodge through the rest of the show. When the last band finished, Damon and a bunch of other counselors took the stage for one last song. "Thanks for making the past two weeks so awesome, everyone," he said. "You're all true rock stars today. You've earned the title. And it may be time to say good-bye, but I hope it's only until next summer."

They began playing "Old Time Rock & Roll," a guaranteed crowd-pleaser. The whole audience got to their feet and started clapping in time. Well, sort of. On either side of me, my musically challenged parents faltered between clapping on two-four and one-three. I clapped louder, hoping they'd pick up the beat from me but knowing they'd lose it again five seconds later. And smiling, because for a moment my family felt like my family again.

I'd come to camp feeling so broken. I didn't feel that way anymore. It was as if all the pieces of me had been unfastened, scattered on the ground, and put back together in a slightly different way. There were a few cogs and springs left over. Yet here I was, still keeping time. No matter what I lost, there'd always be enough of me left to carry on.

One part of my song had been dead wrong. My family hadn't been broken in half, not really. We were three wholes. We always had been.

The houselights came up. The applause petered out. "Well," said Dad, "I guess that's it, huh?"

"I guess it is," I said. Around us, families reconnected and started heading toward the doors. The conversations were already turning away from the show that had just finished and toward everybody's long drive home. Just like that, camp was over.

"Melly!" It was Adeline. I spun to see her hurrying through the crowd toward me. "You weren't seriously going to leave without saying good-bye, were you?"

"Only if I wanted to regret it for the rest of my life," I said.

She threw her arms around me and squeezed so hard I could barely breathe. Or maybe it was the lump that suddenly materialized in my throat. "I don't know if I could've made it through the past two weeks without you," I said, so quietly only she could hear. "Thank you."

"No, thank you," she said, "for making this, hands down, my best summer ever."

"Do we really have to wait three hundred and fifty days to see each other again?" I asked. "It doesn't seem fair."

"It isn't," Adeline said, "but you've got a phone, and I've got a phone, and when we're back in civilization and can actually get a signal . . ."

"I already can't wait," I said.

We hugged one more time, extra long and extra tight. "I don't want to let go," Adeline whispered.

"Me neither," I said, choking up. "On the count of three?"

"On the count of three," Adeline said, "and no crying. Promise?"

We counted to three and let go. Even though Adeline was wearing her trademark smile as she stepped away, her eyes were bright and wet. "See you next summer,

Melly," she said. She turned and ran back to her family.

Five minutes later, Mom and Dad and I were pulling out of the Camp Rockaway parking lot, dust billowing around the car windows. As we whizzed along the roller coaster hills back to the highway, Mom said, "So, this friend of yours. Adeline."

"Yes," Dad said, "tell us about Adeline."

I leaned back in my seat and stretched out my legs, browner than they'd been two weeks ago and dotted with mosquito bites. I scratched an especially itchy one. "I have a better idea," I said. "Why don't I start at the beginning?"

Acknowledgments

A standing ovation for those instrumental in bringing Melly to the stage:

My parents, Gary and Sheila Bigelow, who have been part of this piece da capo al coda—from sponsoring the childhood music lessons and summer camps that inspired Melly's adventures, to last-minute fact-checking.

My talented friends—writers, musicians, and in several cases both—Eliza Butler, Joe Chellman, Rebecca Dudley, Carey Farrell, Carol Coven Grannick, Lis Harvey, and Michelle Sussman, who rehearsed Melly for ~~auditions~~ submissions.

My agent, Steven Chudney, who saw Melly's potential long before she learned to drum and worked doggedly to make her voice heard.

My editor, Jocelyn Davies, and her dizzyingly

detail-oriented team, who heard the truth of Melly's song beyond the false notes and pushed her performance to the next level.

Everyone who requested an encore to *Starting from Here*. It means the world to me.